COME AND HAVE A GO IF YOU THINK YOU'RE **MAD** ENOUGH!

*Are you* **MAD** *enough to collect the series?*

COME AND HAVE A GO IF YOU THINK YOU'RE **SMART** ENOUGH!

COME AND HAVE A GO IF YOU THINK YOU'RE **COOL** ENOUGH!

COME AND HAVE A GO IF YOU THINK YOU'RE **MAD** ENOUGH!

COME AND HAVE A GO IF YOU THINK YOU'RE **RICH** ENOUGH!

# COME AND HAVE A GO IF YOU THINK YOU'RE MAD ENOUGH!

**Haydn Middleton**

Hippo

C406276082

Scholastic Children's Books,
Commonwealth House, 1–19 New Oxford Street,
London, WC1A 1NU, UK
a division of Scholastic Ltd
London ~ New York ~ Toronto ~ Sydney ~ Auckland
Mexico City ~ New Delhi ~ Hong Kong

First published in the UK by Scholastic Ltd, 1999

Text copyright © Haydn Middleton, 1999
Illustrations copyright © Philip Reeve, 1999

ISBN 0 439 01082 9

All rights reserved

Typeset by DP Photosetting, Aylesbury, Bucks
Printed and bound by Bath Press, Bath

1 2 3 4 5 6 7 8 9 10

The rights of Haydn Middleton and Philip Reeve to be
identified respectively as the author and illustrator of this work have
been asserted by them in accordance with the Copyright,
Designs and Patents Act, 1988.

For Rhianedd and Delyth – Nutty enough for anyone's Barmy Army!

**1**

"OK, that's enough! I can't take any more! I've never *seen* such a shambles!"

The voice of Benny Webb – manager of Castle Albion FC – rang out across Ash Acre stadium, bringing first-team training to an end for another Wednesday morning. "And if you lot are plannin' to play like that tonight," Benny yelled on at the team in blue bibs, "we might as well ring Torquay United right now and tell them not to bother coming. We'll *give* 'em the three points!"

The players in white bibs punched the air in triumph. They had just won the eight-a-side practice game by seven goals to nil, and the scorer of three of them – schoolboy midfielder Luke Green – had more reason than most to look pleased. But as he followed everyone off the pitch, he wasn't smiling too hard.

Luke's mind was already on that night's Nationwide League Division Three match against Torquay. It was one that Albion had to win. With twelve games still to play, they were second from bottom of the table. But four of the blue-bibbers – goalie Madman Mort, defenders Craig Edwards and Dennis Meldrum, and striker Carl Davey – were all in the Albion team, and Benny had been right: if they played the same way later, their visitors would walk all over them.

"You in particular," Benny moaned, stabbing a finger at eighteen-year-old Madman as he trudged towards the tunnel. "You were all over the place! At fault for every goal. You're not fit! You're not sharp! You're not *hungry*!"

"Oh, I don't know about that, Boss," said physio Terry Vaudeville. "Look."

And just before the burly keeper passed the dug-outs, he stuck a hand in the back pocket of his droopy tracksuit bottoms, took out a badly squashed, half-eaten chicken-and-mushroom pie, then lovingly sank his teeth into it.

Luke couldn't help grinning. Pretty well everything Madman did made you grin. Either that, or pull your hair out. But the crazy custodian's appetite for junk food was getting out of control. And so was his waistline.

"That lad's eating for England," said Terry, in the tunnel. "The rate he's going, he'll soon be filling up the whole goal."

"Well, that's one way of keeping a clean sheet," grinned YTS trainee Chrissie Pick –

left-sided midfielder and Boy With The Biggest Hair In The Nationwide League. "And it's about the only way *he*'ll ever keep one!"

"It's all very well for you to laugh, Chrissie," said Big Benny, pausing outside the door to the away-team dressing room. "You share digs with the bloke. You ought to be helpin' him out. He must have a problem to be bingeing the way he does."

"Oh, he's definitely got a problem," Chrissie piped straight back. "He's no flipping good in goal. End of story. Ain't that the truth, Frederick?"

The player Chrissie had called out to turned and loped back along the corridor towards them. His name was Frederick Dulac – cool ruler of Albion's defence, Luke's best mate and – like Luke – still a schoolboy. "Whassup?" he asked.

"Benny wants to know what Madman's problem is," Chrissie said. "So I told him – he's rubbish at his job. My *landlady* could stop more shots than him – *and* do her ironing at the same time."

Cool Frederick's eyebrow went up – only a fraction of an inch. Both on the pitch and off it, he didn't like to waste energy. For a long moment everyone looked at him. Then he said just one word. "Penalties."

"He's right there," Luke agreed, and everyone had to nod. "Madman's the best penalty-saver in our League, bar none. Look how brilliant he was saving that spot-kick from Shearer in the last round of the Cup."

More nods. Benny gave his big bushy beard a thoughtful stroke. Amazingly enough, although Albion couldn't beat eggs in the League, they'd stormed their way through to the quarter finals of the FA Cup – knocking out Villa, Wolves and Newcastle along the way. Their reward was a home tie on the following Sunday against mighty Liverpool – Robbie Fowler, Jamie Redknapp, Michael Owen and all. *And* it was going to be shown live on TV!

Benny tugged his beard in bafflement. "What *is* it with the lad?" he asked. "How can he save anything belted at him from twelve yards, then let the softest back-pass beat him all ends up? Why can't he just *concentrate*?" He shrugged his big shoulders inside his trademark sheepskin coat and slumped back against the away-team door.

"Don't do that, Boss!" cried Terry the Physio, lunging forward – but too late.

As soon as Benny's great bulk touched the door it creaked, gave a little wooden scream – and came completely off the wall. Both door and startled manager went crashing to the floor of the away-team dressing room. Terry rushed up, grabbed Benny's hand and hauled him to his feet almost before he realized what had happened.

"What the...?" began the dazed supremo.

"Oh, I've just loosened up the hinges a bit," Terry explained. "Ready for tonight's guests." Terry liked to make life as uncomfortable as possible for any of Ash Acre's visiting teams – fusing the lights, turning off the heating, making sure the toilets didn't flush. Home advantage, he called it.

"Well that's all right then," said Benny, dusting himself down. "But seriously, what are we gonna do about Madman? He's got a problem and he needs some kind of help – and quick. I keep waking up in a cold sweat thinking of him in a one-on-one with Michael Owen. Just think! Owen'll have him for breakfast."

"And elevenses," nodded Chrissie. "And lunch. And tea. And dinner..."

"Oh go spray your hair," Benny scowled at him. Then he turned to Luke and Frederick. "You two, think it over, will you? You're the ones with the brains around here. All I wanna know is this: how are we gonna get Madman concentrating for ninety minutes the way he concentrates for nine-tenths of a second when he's facing up to a pen? There's *got* to be something we can do."

"Right, Boss," said Luke, wondering if George Graham ever came to David Ginola and Sol Campbell with this sort of request. "Er – we'll have a think."

For the rest of that day Luke didn't have much time to think. His headmistress let him out of school for just one training session a week and when he got back she expected him to work twice as hard. It was good of her to let him out at all really. But as an Albion season-ticket holder, she knew how vital Luke and Frederick were. Without them, her team would now be *well* adrift at the foot of the Div Three table – and bang on course for the drop to the Football Conference.

When school finished, Luke's mum was waiting for him outside the gates. Luke's mum was a woman with very clear views on what she liked and didn't like. Her likes were gardening, antiques shops and bossing around Luke's stepdad Rodney. Her dislikes were football, football, football and football. Oh, and football.

It wasn't just the game itself she detested. She couldn't stand the wall-to-wall media coverage either. Or the way everyone from

Prime Ministers to lollipop ladies took it all so *seriously*. Or the ridiculous look and feel of modern-day kits. Or the smell of ghastly-burgers wafting down from Ash Acre on match-days. Or Glenn Hoddle's bad grammar. Or Mark Lawrenson's moustache, just ... *everything*.

She absolutely forbade Luke to watch Castle Albion play. And two months before, she'd gone postal when she found out that her son – Britain's youngest-ever player – was actually in the team. Since then she'd done everything in her power to keep him out of Benny Webb's clutches. As far as she was concerned, she never wanted him to kick a *tin can* again, let alone a football. And as far as she was aware, his budding career was well and truly finished.

But luckily for Luke, not everyone saw things the same way as his manic mum. His dad, stepdad, grandparents and headmistress all knew talent when they saw it – and they wanted Luke to put it to good use. So although his mum escorted him safely home on that March after-noon, his dad had arranged to have him for the night. Which meant that at exactly twenty-past seven, he delivered Luke to Ash Acre, all ready for the big kick-off against Torquay at seven forty-five.

"Sock it to 'em, baby," said his dad, as he dropped him outside the players' entrance. Luke's dad – a deeply unsuccessful singer-guitarist – always spoke like that. It went with his flower-power van, his frazzled-looking ponytail and the hippie gear he'd been wearing for the best part of three decades.

"I'll try, Dad," Luke replied, immediately attracting a flock of autograph-hunters even younger than himself.

"Word's out that Gerard Houllier's gonna be here," his dad went on. "Spying mission for Liverpool. You never know, son. Play your pants off tonight and maybe he'll wanna sign you up for the Reds!"

Luke grinned. "Nah. I'm happy here at Albion." He said the same thing to local reporters every time he was linked with a bigger, richer club. "Besides, it's hard enough getting past mum for the home games *here*. How would I ever get up to Anfield and back twenty-odd times a season?"

Quickly he signed the kids' books and programmes and headed for the dressing room. Along the way club officials patted him on the back and ruffled his hair. "Hat-trick tonight then, Luke?" asked one. "You'll turn this lot over, no sweat," said another. "Bunch of nancies, Torquay," laughed a very tall secretary.

But Luke heard the tension in their voices. Everyone knew that Albion had to start getting it together in the League. For weeks they'd been more scored against than scoring: nil-one to

Darlington, nil-two to Chester City, one-three to Rotherham. On and on it went, with the threat of the Conference looming ever larger. But at least, Luke thought, as he pushed back the dressing-room door, we all know what we've got to do now. We're all in this together. All for one, one for all.

The sight that met him inside made his eyes pop. Up on the physio's bench, four grown men – skipper Gaffer Mann, Narris Phiz the Trinidadian central midfielder, Dennis Meldrum and ex-England veteran Ruel Bibbo – were sitting in a line *on top of* a flattened Madman Mort. And every time he tried frantically to jerk or wriggle free, they all just bounced on him.

"I can't say I blame 'em," Benny shrugged at Luke. "He was making that blessed aeroplane racket of his. Deafening, it was. Couldn't hear ourselves think." Madman could make any number of Plane-Engine Sounds Through The Ages and he liked to prove the point to his teammates on match-days.

"But it's a vital part of my preparation!" Madman complained from under Gaffer Mann's left thigh. "Without it I'll be half the keeper I normally am!"

"Which is about a quarter as good as you *need* to be," Benny spat back. "Now shut it, all of you, get changed, then listen up to what I've got to say."

Within minutes everyone was sitting attentively in their blue-and-white hooped shirts, with their boots laced up tight. All except Luke, that was. Since his mum had never let him own a pair of boots, it was too late now for him to get used to playing on studs. So *he* wore trainers – and even on the softest surfaces he still got higher marks out of ten in the tabloids than any other Nationwide midfielder.

"Right, lads," said Benny, rubbing his hands together. His words of wisdom were usually worth waiting for. "This is the first day of the season..."

A puzzled rumble went round the dressing room. "No it's not, Boss." "What about them thirty-four games we've played already?" "It's *March*, Boss, not August."

"Today," Benny shouted louder. "Is Day One. Of The Season. *Geddit?* This is Year Zero. Today we begin *all over again*. A Fresh Start. A New Beginning. A Completely Clean Sheet..."

"Not with him, it won't be," chorused Narris Phiz and Craig Edwards, both glaring accusingly at Madman.

"For you *especially*, Madman," Benny went on, "this is the first day of the rest of your career. From here on in, I want you to concentrate, concentrate, concentrate. Now everyone – get out on that pitch and Play Smart Football!"

Led by the Gaffer, the players sprang to their

feet, dragged back the door and charged up the tunnel. At exactly the same time, the Torquay team next door tried to do likewise. But with a great dull thud, *their* door fell in on top of them. As Luke glanced back at the mayhem it caused, he found Terry the Physio right behind him.

"Lovely job," whispered Terry with a wink.

**3**

Once they'd got their door back up, the visitors took a while to settle. Their hundred and fifty intrepid travelling fans gave them a fair bit of stick about it too. But to be fair, Albion weren't giving Torquay much of a chance to impress. For the first twenty-five minutes *they* looked more like the side currently lying fifth in the table. And in the twenty-sixth minute they got their reward by taking the lead.

Narris and the Torquay number seven got into a bit of argy-bargy on the halfway line. Six of one, half a dozen of the other. But Albion got the free kick. Luke trotted over to place the ball, and noticed that one full-back was defending very deep. Without even taking a run-up, he lashed in a cross at head-height towards the far post. Ruel had already snaked away from his marker – who loudly appealed for offside. But that full-back was keeping Ruel *on*. The big man kept going, met Luke's cross just inside the six-yard box and powered a header into the net.

**"We Love You, Al-bi-on, Oh Yes We Do!"**
the home faithful in the 2,476 crowd erupted. For fans and players alike, it was an unusual experience to be ahead. But they had to start getting used to it – because in the thirty-eighth minute, the Green-Bibbo combination struck for a second time.

Again the poor Torquay number two was involved. After a corner he made a horlicks of a clearance on the edge of the box – slicing it straight out wide to Luke. This time the Studless Sensation drove the ball back in so hard that the merest touch from anyone would have diverted it over the line. That touch came from Ruel.

**"You're The Greatest Team**
**The World Has Ever Seen!"**
chanted the Albion South Side – with perhaps just a trace of exaggeration. The Torquay travellers, meanwhile, weren't being quite so complimentary about their number two.

When the ref blew his whistle for sweet tea and tactical updates, everyone attached to Albion could look back with satisfaction on their best first half for yonks.

"See, I *told* you!" Benny blared in the dressing room. "Year Zero! This is where we start to go places. We've got our act together now and no mistake."

"Old Gerard Houllier *is* up in the stand,"

Gaffer Mann nodded, blowing on his tea. "He'll have enjoyed that little display!"

"He must be wetting himself," roared Michael "Half-Fat" Milkes, the man with the midfield holding role. "They're not gonna take Fortress Albion. Not Torquay, not Liverpool, *not no one*!"

"Nice goals too, Ruel," chirped Terry the Physio.

"Yeah, that doubled your total for the season, didn't it?" smirked Carl Davey, ducking before Ruel could clip his ear. Big Mr Bibbo then grinned sideways at Luke. Long, long ago he'd been one of the first black strikers to wear an England shirt. He'd even scored in a World Cup qualifier. Now he was well and truly into the twilight of his career. And it was true that he'd been having trouble finding the net of late. But a brace of goals before half-time puts a spring in the step of any striker. In fact everyone in the room was on Cloud Nine. Only Madman sat quietly – which was about as rare as a dog getting up on its hind legs and unlocking the front door when it wants to go for a pee.

"What's up, Morty?" Benny asked. "I thought you had a smashin' first half. Safe pair of hands on the crosses. Good bit of length on your kicks. Couple of nice throw-outs to Luke and Frederick."

Madman just fiddled with his cap. "I should've done my full pre-match preparation," he muttered to the floor. "I don't feel right. I'm not quite *on* it."

As everyone then tried to buck him up, he unfolded the cap and, in the sudden stunned silence, produced a rancid-looking kebab, still on its skewer. Before anyone could protest, he held it up above his mouth and *shook* the lumps of fatty meat, peppers, mushrooms and burnt onions into the bottomless pit below.

"I dunno about 'on' it," whined Carl Davey, wincing. "*I* feel right *off* it now."

At that moment the door opened and Ron Sainty, the club's longest-serving director, popped his head round. He didn't look too happy. Then again, Mr Sainty never did. Despite the successful Cup-run, Albion's debts were enormous. The club swallowed money like Madman swallowed Pot Noodles. And rumours were now going round that official sponsors Lampshades Plus were about to pull out. "A word in your ear, Benny?" he said. "Up in the box."

"All right then, lads," said Benny before slipping out. "More of the same for the next forty-five, eh? I predict five-nothing."

But if Benny ever got red-carded from Ash Acre, he had no future as a Mystic Ex-manager.

Behind their wonky door, Torquay had got themselves well sorted. Fitted out with a new formation, they came at Albion like a pack of Devon demons after the break, twice hitting Madman's bar within ten minutes.

Both times the keeper was beaten all ends up – and when he was beaten a third time, no woodwork came to his rescue. It wasn't even a shot. Just a high, hopeful cross to the far post. Completely unchallenged, Madman went up to collect, somehow forgot to close both hands on the ball, and finally it was Craig Edwards who collected the thing – from inside the back of the Albion net.

That sparked a bit of an Albion revival. Luke and Frederick did all they could to get their first-half passing rhythm back. They won a couple of corners, and Carl went close with a solo run on goal. But when a keeper makes a booboo like Madman's, it stays in his team-mates' minds. And in the seventy-seventh minute he made well and truly sure they didn't forget it – by doing it all over again!

This time it came after a slick end-to-end move down Torquay's right flank. The feeble full-back who had gifted Albion both their goals was now a new man. Literally. His manager had subbed him at half-time, and his replacement was more of a winger than a defender. After playing three one-twos down the touchline, he got in behind Gaffer but stubbed his toe as he whacked in his shot. Madman didn't seem to notice how slowly the ball was coming his way. He dived before it arrived, watched it bounce, half-scrambled to his feet then dived back again – but with his hands too far apart. In went the equalizer.

Torquay sniffed victory now. In the last thirteen minutes everyone in their side peppered Madman's goal with shots. Typically, the inconsistent keeper now pulled off a string of blinding saves. But his new-found concentration didn't last. The ref had his whistle in his mouth as the Torquay goalie punted the ball upfield. The Albion defence had pushed up to halfway, the ball sailed over everyone and bounced twelve yards short of the penalty box. Madman dashed out to head clear. But a moment too late. He timed his jump all wrong, headed the ball *backwards* – and up it looped into his own net for the Torquay winner.

Luke had never heard a football crowd fall so silent – apart from the hundred and fifty triumphant travellers from Torquay.

"You're past your play-by date!" Narris snarled at Madman once they were all back inside. "*Well* past it!" More of the same followed, in slightly more fruity language, from several of the others.

All Madman could do was sit and look at the

inside of his cap. He knew he'd made a pig's ear of things.

Luke couldn't help feeling sorry for him. After all, he *was* the best keeper they'd got. (Or rather, the only one.) And there wasn't even a bit of pie or old fishfinger for him to chew on. Or so it seemed...

Madman still had one more surprise up his sleeve. Reaching inside his left cuff, he dragged out a fistful of congealed spaghetti and stuffed it into his mouth.

"Diabolical!" boomed Benny, sweeping into the room in a sheepskin blur.

"It's only pasta left over from lunch, Boss," Madman mumbled gloomily.

"I'm not talking about you! This is somethin' even worse – if that's possible."

"Don't tell us," Stuart sighed. "Shrewsbury have won? We're bottom?"

"Not that either. The club's got a cash-flow crisis. There's nothing in the kitty." He took a breath. "And they're stopping *all* our wages till further notice."

**4**

When Luke came out of school the next afternoon, he expected to find Rodney his stepdad
waiting for him. His mum had a gardening class
and she didn't trust Luke to go straight home
without getting lured back into the seedy world
of soccer. She knew that in the past, seedy
soccer people had lain in wait for him at the
school gates. And to her way of thinking, they
didn't come any seedier than players' agent
Neil Veal.

Vealy already represented Chrissie Pick and
Madman Mort. The rest of his roster consisted
of male strippers, kiss-and-tell bimbos and Noel
Edmonds lookalikes. For weeks he'd been
chasing both Luke and Frederick in an attempt
to add some real class to his list. He'd even tried
to tempt Luke with a complimentary pair of
Adidas Predators – which Luke's mum had
immediately slung with fearsome accuracy at
Veal's heavily-gelled and Raybanned head.

But there was no sign today of Agent Veal's

silver-grey BMW convertible. Just Rodney standing out on the street and – right behind him – Benny Webb.

Now what Luke's mum didn't know was that Rodney and Benny were working in tandem to make sure Luke played in as many Albion games as possible. Rodney might have *looked* like a complete prannit. And all he *seemed* to be interested in was spotting birds, country and western music, and stopping Luke's mum from blowing her fusebox on a daily basis. But deep beneath his purple puffer jacket there beat the heart of a rock-solid footie fan.

In his own quiet way, Rodney had done it all: cried with pride in front of his black-and-white telly when England won the World Cup in 1966, never missed a single home game at non-League Purfleet between 1975 and 1981, been lightly beaten up by marauding Norwich City fans at an M6 service station in 1983, driven to Liverpool to lay flowers after the terrible Hillsborough tragedy of 1989 – and Luke's mum didn't have the faintest inkling about *any* of it.

"Luke," he called out now, blinking behind his glasses, "Mr Webb wants a word. He says it's pretty urgent." Benny looked on, ashenfaced, over his shoulder. Even his sheepskin collar looked mournful.

"What is it, Boss?" Luke asked. "If it's about the pay-freeze, it doesn't bother me too much, to be honest. My dad has to look after whatever money I earn. He puts it in a trust for me and I haven't even seen any of it yet."

Benny shook his head. "That's a good attitude, son, and I appreciate it. And of course it don't matter a jot to me neither. I love this club – and I'll work for nothing for as long as it takes. Some of them others, though – they don't think it's too clever. It's bound to have an effect on team morale."

"So is losing three-two at home to Torquay after being two-nil up," quipped a wise-guy from Luke's class who was listening-in by the dustbins with a gang of others.

Benny threw a pained look their way, then shepherded Luke and Rodney a little further up the street. They stopped next to his battered silver Volvo.

"Well," said Luke, to cheer him up, "my dad's doing a gig at The Third Way next Thursday, and he said last night that he was prepared to donate all the takings to Albion's Fighting Fund – turn it into a charity concert."

Benny looked touched. "Good for him. We've all got to pitch in now. But look, the money stuff ain't the main reason I've stopped off here today to see you. It's more about this Madman business. We've *gotta* get him sorted. Any team is only as good as its last line of defence..."

He pulled a crumpled sheaf of exercise-book

pages from his coat pocket. "Look – I've typed up these diet sheets for the lad. He's got to get some discipline into his eating. You know what they say: You Are What You Eat."

Luke glimpsed the top page and sensed that Benny wasn't right at the cutting edge of the science of calorie control. *Friday Dinner*, it said, *Steak-and-kidney pie, chips but NO mushy peas.* "But that's only a part of it. We've got to get his head right too. Like I told you yesterday, Luke, he needs something to bring back his confidence in open play. I asked you to have a think about it. Any luck yet?"

Luke frowned. "Well, I did have a *sort* of idea."

"Send him to a therapist?" suggested Rodney. "Put him through a course of psychoanalysis?"

"We haven't got time for anything like that," said Benny. "Not unless they do brain transplants on the NHS."

"No," said Luke. "It was simpler than that. I just thought that – well – maybe Madman needs to think of his net as a kind of *sacred* place. The kind of place he would do *anything* to stop someone scoring in…"

"I'm not with you, son," Benny said. "You mean turn his goal into a church?"

"That wouldn't work," smiled Mr Beavon, the woodwork teacher, as he strode by. "He doesn't like crosses."

"No," Luke explained. "I just wondered if Madman couldn't *make* his goal a sacred place by putting something inside it that he really treasured."

"A Pizza Hut menu?" Rodney suggested, not meaning to be funny.

"Something he'd want to defend with his life," Luke went on. "A framed photo of a close relative perhaps. A cuddly toy he'd loved as a toddler. Something that really matters *to him*." He shrugged. "It was just a thought."

Benny and Rodney let this sink in. Then both men began to nod. "You know," Benny said, "I like the sound of that. Could you come over with me now to Madman's digs? I think he might react better to the idea if it came from you."

Rodney hopped from foot to foot like a con-stipated starling. "Ooh, er – I do have to get Luke home. His mum'll soon be back from her gardening class..."

"Tomorrow, though," Luke cut in, "I'm going to Frederick's after school. To work on some maths problems with him. Madman lives quite close by. I could nip round then with Frederick. OK?"

"OK," beamed Benny. "Magic." Then from across the road half a dozen kids pointed their way and bellowed:

**"You're Goin' Down To The Football Con-fer-ence!"**

"Or maybe we're not," Benny said softly to Luke. "Especially if you can get old Madman back up to speed."

Luke's mum dropped him at Frederick's house at ten-to-four on Friday. She said she would come back and pick him up in precisely two hours. Luke did a quick mental sum. He reckoned they could get the maths done and dusted in about ninety mins. That would give them a good half-hour to scoot round to Madman and Chrissie's digs on their sort-out-the-sloppy-keeper mission.

Frederick was already home. In fact, he'd been home all day. Luke wasn't sure how the arrangement had started, but the school let Cool F come and go pretty much as he pleased. He lived with his older sister, and seemed to spend most of his time running a rare records search service – a nice little earner for him. But the work he handed in to his teachers was always right up there on a par with his performances in a Castle Albion shirt: straight A's all the way for style, content and sheer cool mastery. And on that Friday afternoon, his input helped to sort the maths problems in just over an hour – then they jogged off together to touch base with the nutty netminder.

The tree-fringed, bay-windowed semi where Madman hung out was pretty posh-looking. Luke could just imagine a hallway with elegant tables and big-leafed plants on a polished wooden floor. And when the little landlady opened the front door, that was exactly what he and Frederick saw behind her. The rest of the house too, from what they could see, was all very spick and span.

"Hello," said Luke brightly. "We've come to see ... Madman." He frowned, feeling a bit silly, but he genuinely didn't know the keeper's first name. No one did. Madman always reckoned he'd lost it. (Or eaten it, according to Narris.)

The woman's face seemed to wobble. She looked from Luke to Frederick then back to Luke again. Her mouth opened but she seemed incapable of speech. Then a little man came out of the front room to stand beside her. "What's all this then?" he asked, not particularly unpleasantly.

"We've come to see Madman," Luke repeated. "Is he in, please?"

At once the man's right cheek twitched. Then it twitched again, seeming to yank his neat, pencil-thin moustache halfway up his face.

"In?" he echoed. "*In?* Well, what do you think *that* is?"

He reached out and grabbed Luke's elbow – quite hard for a little guy – pulled him into the house and pointed up the thickly-carpeted stairs. Puzzled at first, Luke didn't know how to answer. Then he heard a faint drone – unmistakable even from down here: Madman, revving up for his impersonation of a Liberator Bomber. Within moments he was at full fearsome throttle – making the tassles on the stair curtains dance and sending the twitch on the landlord's face into fifth gear. Even so, Luke could tell this wasn't Madman at his old carefree best. There was a melancholy edge to the blitz of sound, a streak of sorrow running through the din. It was plain for all to hear – this was not a happy aeroplane.

"He's a nice enough lad," the landlord said, letting Luke go, "but why does he have to do *that*? It's driving us *barmy*!" Luke heard his wife softly close the front door, and Frederick pad up behind him. Then the landlord narrowed his eyes at them both. "Hey – that agent chappie hasn't sent you, has he?"

"Agent? No." Obviously this guy wasn't a member of the Neil Veal fan club either. "We're just team-mates."

"Go on then. Up you go. But for pity's sake, tell him to put a sock in it."

Luke and Frederick climbed the stairs to the eye of the storm. When they tapped on the back-bedroom door, it was like trying to make a burp heard at a Spice Girls concert. Already Luke guessed that *this* room was going to be different from the rest of the house. Little things suggested it. The smell seeping out, for instance. Like the school dinner-hall on a boiled-cabbage day, shot through with the pong of ancient fried cod, lashings of Brylcreem and more than a hint of long-unwashed sock. Then there was the *other* sound: in between the ever-louder engine roars – a CD track by the Prodigy, Chrissie's top band, and that too was rising in volume all the time, as if in competition.

Frederick leaned past Luke and rapped harder. The engine noise ceased. The song was turned down. Luke even fancied that the sock stink grew fainter. "Step inside!" cried out a high-pitched voice that could only have been Chrissie's.

Luke and Frederick looked at each other before turning the handle. But once the door was open, they didn't step inside. They couldn't. There just wasn't enough space. The floor was a sea of fast-food cartons and hair-care aerosols. There were two beds, and between them there seemed to be a third, consisting entirely of dirty clothes, magazines, Coke cans and a mass of saggy balloons.

"Why!" yelled Madman from on top of this pile. "It's the Studless Sensation and the Cool Ruler!" He was wearing his full goalkeeping kit. He was *always* wearing his full goalkeeping kit. Sometimes even in the after-match bath.

"Welcome to our 'umble abode," grinned Chrissie, looking up from under his teetering pile of hair. He was perched on the end of the nearer bed, writing a slogan in black biro on the white T-shirt he was planning to wear under the blue-and-white hoops against Liverpool. If and when he scored a goal, he would hoik up his top shirt – Ian Wright-style – to reveal this homemade message to the adoring Albion faithful. Luke couldn't read upside down, but Frederick could. He gestured at the last word. "That's H-A-I-R," he said.

"What?" cried Chrissie, screwing up his face. He held up his handiwork for the visitors to see more clearly. *I Love My Hare*, the T-shirt proudly proclaimed. Seeing it through their eyes, he noticed his mistake. "Oh – *FLIP!*" he sighed, tossing the shirt behind him into the between-bed pile, yanking out another that looked more or less white, and beginning to block in a new slogan.

"So anyway," Madman cried. "To what do we owe the pleasure of this visit?"

"We, er, we were just in the area," Luke began. As he did so, the front doorbell rang again. "We thought we'd just look in..." ("Not today thank you," barked the landlord down below. "Not *any* day!" Then Luke heard him slam the door shut.)

"Shall I do an impression?" Madman asked, waving at an array of poorly-painted Airfix aircraft hanging on cotton threads from the ceiling behind him. "A Sopwith Camel? Something from the Mitsubishi fighter range?"

"Whoa!" Frederick said, raising a hand to show that this was *not* a good idea.

"Or we could play Beat The Keeper." Madman bent down and tugged a balloon free from the pile. He patted it over towards Luke, who dutifully headed it back. It was going straight to Madman but he took a step to his left, dived right, caught the balloon in his midriff, then crashed down on to his own bed. "*Supersave!*" he shouted, raising one gloved hand.

Down below, the bell rang once again. Right away Luke heard the front door being torn back. "I'm warning you!" growled the man with the twitch. "We don't want your sort round here. You're a low-down spiv with no sense of values and you shouldn't be allowed near impressionable young men. Now get lost!" *Slam!* The whole house seemed to judder.

"As it happens," Luke said hesitantly to Madman, "we'd, er, been wanting to make a sort of suggestion about your goalkeeping."

"I make suggestions about it all the time," chuckled Chrissie Pick, not looking up from his T-shirt.

"No, no. It's not critical," Luke said quickly. "It's just an idea. Something that might make you an even *better* keeper than you already are."

"Oh yeah?" Madman was still heaped on the bed, clutching his balloon. And Luke was still taking in the full horror of the room. You Are What You Eat, Benny had said. In that case Madman was a Kentucky Fried Chicken with chewed-up burger buns for wings and a pair of Mars Bars for legs. Luke also saw Benny's diet sheets, blu-tacked above the dressing-table mirror, next to pics of Elvis Presley, Dolly Parton and several other Big Hair icons – plus a mug-shot of the Prodigy's Keef, who of course, had almost no hair at all.

"What about this, though?" Luke bashed on. "Just tell me what you think..."

He launched into an easy-to-follow outline of his scheme to turn Madman's goal into a no-go area for flying footballs. "So you see," he rounded it off, "it might make you *extra* determined to keep the ball out of the net."

"In open play," Frederick murmured.

"Oh absolutely," Luke said fast. "Not that you'd need it when you're facing up to pens. *No one*'s better than you at saving shots from the spot."

Madman's face went dark. It tended to do that when he concentrated. Which wasn't very often. So the look of him now was a bit scary. Was he upset? Or even outraged? Or was he just thinking, hard, about what he could put in the back of his net? Luke wasn't fated to find out right away.

Yet again the *dah-de-dah* of the front doorbell rang out. "Hey!" Chrissie grinned, jumping up and throwing his shirt and biro aside. "I reckon I know who that's got to be down there. Only one bloke would *keep* coming back!"

"It's our main man!" agreed Madman, leaping up himself. Both guys dashed out of the room, passing the startled Luke and Cool F, before peering down over the landing banister. The two younger lads followed and looked curiously over their shoulders. "Don't touch the hair!" hissed Chrissie at once, and Luke backed off a shade.

Out came the landlord for the third time. As he stomped down the hall, Luke thought he could see even the top of his bald head twitching. "*This*'ll put the cat among the pygmies," whispered Chrissie. And he wasn't wrong.

Luke had heard of foot-in-the-door merchants before: never-say-die travelling salesmen who wedge one foot between front door and doorway to stop the home-owner from giving them the bum's rush. But never, before this moment, had he heard of a *head*-in-the-door tactic. Yet here, directly below, there unfolded a mini-masterclass in this previously obscure art.

As soon as the landlord pulled back the door, just twelve inches or so, and wound himself up to hurl abuse at the persistent caller, the man in question poked his head through the gap. The next bit happened very fast. Surprised by the gambit, the landlord did two things. First he tried to force the door back. Second, in doing this, his own face went forward. The twin result was that the caller got his neck jammed tight *and* got his nose nutted by the landlord's shiny head. "Double-*whammy*!" breathed a mightily-impressed Chrissie Pick.

Wincing, Luke looked away. But when he looked again, the two men seemed to be frozen in combat. For reasons best known to himself, the landlord was still pushing the door hard, so the caller couldn't pull out his damaged head and neck even if he wanted to. Then Luke looked closer – and he saw that this head and neck were familiar. Very much so, as John Motson would say. Gelled hair, wonky Ray-bans, a constellation of pimples and – even now – the sleaziest grin this side of Soho. It was Neil Veal – players' agent!

Of course! He must have been out stalking – and finding all four lads in the same house had been just too good an opportunity to miss. And a little matter like having his head stuck wasn't going to stop him from cashing in on it. Grog-gily his eyes swivelled up and brought the four players' faces into focus.

"Great to catch you guys!" he grunted. "Hey, Chrissie – I'm *this close* to a Wash & Go deal for you." The landlord – silent, twitching – pushed harder. Veal gave what sounded like a death-rattle. "Luke, Frederick – we should talk. Let's do..." his eyes went blurry under the door's pressure, "...a takeaway ... sometime."

At last the landlord wised up, pulled back the door, and Veal's head disappeared like the cork shooting out of a bottle of fizz. Mr Twitch slammed the door, turned and marched off.

"Radical," remarked Cool Frederick, and the other three nodded.

"Look," said Luke. "We should go too." Keen

to avoid more contact with the landlord, he skipped downstairs and opened the front door. Agent Veal's BMW was just wobbling away. "We'll see you on Sunday," he called back up, with Frederick right behind him.

"Bring on those Scousers!" grinned Madman, rubbing his gloves. "And that idea of yours, Luke. Putting the thingy in the goal? I like it. I'm gonna do it!"

"Safe," smiled Luke. And even before he and Frederick were out of the front garden they could hear Madman – deep in the bowels of his hellhole of a bedroom – breaking into his unmistakable version of a DC10 circling Gatwick.

**7**

Luke didn't get much sleep on Saturday night. Normally he slept soundly before big games but, to be fair, he'd never taken part in a game *this* big before. Liverpool at home in the FA Cup Quarter-Final! Games just didn't come much bigger – certainly not for penniless little outfits like Castle Albion.

As Luke rode his bike up to the stadium after lunch on Sunday, he saw an awestruck look on all the home fans' faces too. This wasn't the 2,476 diehards who'd turned up for the Torquay Turnaround. This was Capacity Crowdsville (13,500 paying customers *plus* the thousand more that the club would cram in illegally and 'forget' to add into the attendance figure).

All the punters in blue and white looked as if they wanted to be pinched. Was this a dream? Were Castle Albion *really* one of only eight clubs left in the world's oldest knockout competition? And did they have any chance against lofty Liverpool – five times winners of the thing, not to mention finishing champions of England *eighteen* times, and with four European Cups thrown in for good measure? Luke's lips went dry just thinking about it. But at least he hadn't had to scramble about to get to this game. His mum's gardening class had gone off on a field trip to an "arboretum", whatever that was. She'd left him a table-full of silver to polish in her absence. But Rodney had agreed to do it for him – while watching the biggest game in Albion's one hundred and twenty-eight-year history live on BBC1.

"Good to see you, son," cried Benny as Luke entered the dressing room. He never quite believed his star player was going to arrive until he actually showed up. "You didn't see Madman on the way in, did you?"

"No, Boss." Luke glanced at his watch. "He's usually here before now, right?"

"Yeah, and giving us a right ear-bashing too," said Craig. "This is miles better."

"I reckon it was that idea of yours, Luke," grinned Dennis. "Benny told us all about it. Madman's probably bringing a hot-dog van to stick in the net, and he's got caught up in all the traffic!"

"Shut up about Madman and get your kit on, lads," Benny told them. "He'll already have *his* kit on when he gets here, so no sweat there." But he didn't sound very convinced, and he didn't look it either. Nor did most of the others as they all prepared in their own special ways for the ninety minutes ahead. This included Craig Edwards hurling a real pineapple at Carl Davey's bottom. The striker always swore it helped him to score. But since he hadn't hit the net for five weeks, the others were starting to wonder if he just enjoyed the pain.

With twenty minutes to kick-off, Madman still hadn't made an appearance. The home dressing room was eerily quiet. So quiet, they could hear Paul Ince geeing up the Reds next door – and punching the wall to keep in practice.

Then it happened. Slowly the door opened inwards. But no face popped around it. For a moment Luke thought it might be Vealy – understandably cautious now about where he stuck his neck. It wasn't him, though. It was Madman: coming in very, very slowly – and backwards.

"Oh no," moaned Ruel. "He's lost all sense of direction. We've had it now!"

Benny, just as perplexed as the next man, reached out to hold the door wide open. Madman backed right in, and then with a flourish turned around. Everyone gasped. Even Paul Ince paused to take a breath and stopped whacking the wall. Cradled in Madman's arms was the biggest, most beautifully-decorated scale model of an aeroplane that Luke had ever seen.

"I had to walk here with it," the keeper purred. "I couldn't risk taking it on a crowded bus. It's a Gloster Gladiator. British World War Two. This was the plane Roald Dahl was flying when he got shot down over Libya. But no one's gonna shoot *this* baby down!"

"Flippin' heck, Madman," said Narris, standing up to get a closer look. "Did you make that? I didn't think you had it in you. It's brilliant."

Madman shook his head. "No, my great-uncle did it. He was RAF himself."

"Airfix kit, was it?" Half-Fat asked, standing too and putting out a hand.

"*Airfix!*" Madman exploded, jerking it out of his reach. "Get a life! It's wood. Wood and glass. He did all this with his own bare hands. This is a complete one-off. There ain't another one like it in the whole wide world. My gran gave it to me when I was six. It's sacred – and so's my goal gonna be when I hang it up from the back stanchion. Just let *anyone* try and touch it!"

Luke glanced worriedly at Benny. The Big Boss Man glanced worriedly back. They were obviously thinking exactly the same thing. Luke had to speak up.

"Er – it's a fantastic model, Madman," he said. "Absolutely unbelievable. But it's – well – pretty *big*, isn't it?"

"I mean, son," Benny put in. "Won't it be a bit

of a big *target* for the opposition? I think young Luke here had something a bit smaller in mind."

Madman seemed not to hear. He just smiled serenely down at his lucky charm. His baby. If he could have put a dummy in its mouth and sung it off to sleep, he would have done so then and there. Luke could see his mind was made up. They would all just have to go with this. But it really was so ... *BIG*.

"OK, OK!" Benny called, bringing everyone to order. Team-talk time. All eyes turned his way. "I'm not gonna lie to you. That lot in next door are better than you. They play better, they look better – and they almost certainly smell better. Individually and collectively they're off a different planet. So only a nutcase would think you can get a result out of this one." He paused, took two great lungfuls of breath and stood a foot taller. "Lads, I AM THAT NUTCASE! Today is gonna be *your* day – I can't say why, I just feel it in my water."

Just then a gigantic hullaballoo broke out in next door. "What's that, Terry?" asked Stuart Mann with a knowing smile.

"Oh, I just had a go at their washbasins. Should flood the whole place out."

*"Now get yourselves out on to that pitch!"* Benny resumed at top volume himself. *"And SWAMP them Premier League prannies!"*

**8**

Some teams need a goal to settle them down. Two goals, and they start to feel nice and comfortable. Three, they get out their slippers and open the cigar-box. Over the years, Liverpool have enjoyed many a three-goal cushion before the first forty-five minutes are up. It's part and parcel of being a sleek, lean-and-mean, internationally-famous superclub. Any player who pulls on the legendary red shirt almost *expects* to pile on the goals now and then – especially against deadbeat Division Three no-hopers like Castle Albion.

What they *don't* expect, however, is to go in at the break three goals *down* to such a scummy bunch. But that – phenomenally – was what they had to do at Ash Acre when the ref blew for half-time. If the home club had been able to afford an electronic scoreboard, it would have read: *Albion 3 Liverpool 0*. Instead, the stadium announcer decided to broadcast the mind-boggling news:

"After the first period *crack, phut*, ladies and gentlemen, the score *fizz, pop, fizz* is Castle Albion three *crackle, hummmmm...*" He got no further. The always-dodgy tannoy went dead. But it didn't matter. Every Albion fan in the crowd blared out the rest of the message for him: *"Liverpool Nil!"* And as he left the pitch, Luke didn't think he'd ever heard so many people laughing so loud and so long in sheer disbelief and utter ecstacy.

Benny personally sheep-hugged each player who entered the dressing room. There were tears in his eyes at the start. By the end they were rolling freely into his beard. The last one in was Madman. (It'd taken him a while to untie the string and take down his Gloster Gladiator from the stanchion.) Benny went to hug him but he backed off at once, afraid the plane might get crushed.

"It's working though, Madman, isn't it?" Benny twinkled, drying his eyes. "You had a stonkin' first half out there. Never seen you so confident." He turned to the rest of the players. "Never seen *any* of you so ... *wonderful...*"

"Look out," grinned Ruel, sipping his tea, "he's gonna start blubbing again."

"Yeah, well never mind about that," said Terry, barging into the room with a portable TV under his arm, putting it on his bench and plugging it in. "Benny don't need to say nothing – let's let *these* fellas do all the talkin'." And up on the screen, the face of Desmond Lynam came into view. Everyone cheered.

"Martin," said a shocked-looking Des, turning to his panel, "you've played in a couple of Cup upsets in your time. What do you make of this?"

Martin O'Neill lurched forward, opened his mouth, and for a split second the impossible seemed to have happened. He was speechless! But no. False alarm. "Castle Albion were ab-so-lute-ly mag-nif-i-cent," he began, thumping himself on the chest and shaking his head. "I cannot remember ever seeing a lower-division side play with such aplomb in a match of such significance..."

"What's that about plums?" asked Carl. "Pineapples, yes. But why plums?"

"*Sssssshhhhh!*" They were showing a replay of the first goal.

"The way young Luke Green takes on Babb here and just leaves him for dead – it's breathtaking. And there now, he looks up before making the cross, notices the keeper just a fraction off his line ... and chips it so delightfully over his head that if *that* isn't Goal of the Season, then I'll take a vow of silence!"

Everyone in the dressing room jumped up to acclaim Luke's masterly opener. And before they sat down, goal number two was being shown again. "Talk us through this one, Trevor," said Des.

"Ten quid on him saying 'West Ham'!" cried Dennis. No one took the bet.

"We-e-e-ll," bleated Mr Brooking, "You were *just* starting to wonder whether maybe the excitement of the early goal *might* lead Castle Albion to lose their composure – and up steps this *highly* promising sweeper Frederick Dulac... I have to say he reminds me *very* strongly of the lad down at West Ham – Rio Ferdinand." Everyone groaned. "He plays this lovely one-two with Ruel Bibbo, and the *power* of that shot from the edge of the box! The keeper didn't see it!"

"*YESSS!*" cheered the half-time heroes in hoops.

"But the whole Albion team has been fantastic, hasn't it?" asked Des. "And due to the financial crisis here at Ash Acre, they're not even getting paid at the moment. Maybe you could try that with your boys, Martin? Anyway, to round it all off, Carl Davey then got on the end of this Chrissie Pick corner. It was a bit of a muddle on the line – shame Alan Hansen isn't here to comment on the defending – but Davey finally guided it home."

"*Get in there, you beauty!*" roared Carl, leaping up to do a shimmy and point meaningfully at his bottom as the others hollered and dragged him back down.

"Meanwhile at the other end," Trevor Brooking continued, "goalkeeper Mort – who lots of people said *might* be the Albion weak spot – has been a real tower of strength..." Three clips followed, showing Madman coming out to save at the feet of Michael Owen, tipping a Jamie Redknapp screamer over the bar, and then untying his precious aeroplane before coming in for the interval.

"Reckon he's flying high there today, eh Martin?" said Des.

"Oh, undoubtedly. The sky's the limit for *all* these boys now."

"Indeed it is," sobbed Benny, pulling out the TV plug and stepping proudly in front of his bunch of giant-killers-in-the-making. "Back you go now, lads. There's nothing more for me to say." But as they left, he called out after them: "Just remember this: I want to be bawling my eyes out at the *end* as well!"

Luke trotted back up the tunnel with the Boss's words ringing in his ears. Knowing Castle Albion, it was a pretty safe bet that Big Blubbery Benny *would* be in tears after the full ninety minutes – one way or another.

In the second half Liverpool had a mountain to climb. Twelve minutes into it, a red mist descended and Paul Ince left the expedition.

The England man had been getting the run-around from Half-Fat Milkes all afternoon. Luke could see Incey glaring harder and harder at his inspired opposite number. Then Carl went up for a Chrissie Pick cross just inside the Liverpool penalty area. He managed to drop a header back into the path of Half-Fat, who suddenly had a clear sight of goal. He drew back his right leg to take aim but before he could swing it forward, Paul the Appalling slid in.

Ex-Albion hard man Chopper Foggon used to *dream* of tackles like this. Ince's right boot caught Half-Fat just above the knee. His left scythed him so high that he ripped the Albion man's shorts – and came close to leaving him absolutely Fat-Free. When everyone in the stadium opened their eyes again Houllier's

Hooligan was on his way off for an early bath. The Reds were down to ten.

Twenty minutes later, after a period of exhibition passing from Albion, the Cup minnows slotted home a fourth goal. Madman came out fearlessly to intercept a through-ball then threw it straight to Frederick wide on the right. Cool F took out three Liverpudlians with an angled cross-field pass to Chrissie, who first-timed it inside to Narris Phiz. Narris burned off Patrik Berger, but instead of arrowing in on goal, he backheeled it to the oncoming Luke.

Keeper David James, ten yards off his line, began to scamper back – sure that Luke would try to chip him again. But he hadn't seen Ruel stealing in at the far post. Luke *did* see him. He flicked over the most delicious cross, Ruel leapt high – and gobbled it up as greedily as Madman Mort unleashed on a sack of pork scratchings. His bullet header bulged the net as poor James toppled over. Four-nil to the Basement Boys.

"The scorer *phizz, kerrang, kaputtt!*" was all the announcer could manage as the Albion team went into celebration-overdrive. But as if with one voice, the crowd finished it off: "...*of Castle Albion's fourth goal of the afternoon was number nine – RUEL BIBBO!*"

From that point on, it was a matter of playing out time. Liverpool were six feet under. After this, they would just have to concentrate on securing a place in the Champions League.

As the game entered its final minute, Luke glanced around to savour the whole historic occasion. This, surely, was as good as it got. *I was there*, misty-eyed people would say to their grandchildren about the day when Albion blew Liverpool out of the water (even if they'd only seen it on TV).

The crowd was raising the roof of the run-down old stadium:

**"Albion! Castle Albion! We'll Support You Evermore!"**

Down in the dug-out, the subs were ankle-deep in Benny Webb's tears of pride. You couldn't buy a moment like this (and in cash-strapped Albion's case you couldn't have afforded it anyway.) The ref looked at his watch. Was it all over?

Not quite. Michael Owen got a rare sniff of the ball and tried a run on goal. Dennis Meldrum wasn't buying that. Expertly he shepherded him out towards the corner flag, then tricked him into putting the ball behind for a goal kick.

Still no whistle. Madman trotted across to fetch the ball and placed it for the goal kick. Usually if he played it short, he looked for Luke or Frederick. But now Dennis, fresh from out-witting young SuperMichael, had his arm raised. Madman duly drilled a perfect ground-pass his way. Dennis trapped it, turned, saw

Michael Owen in front of him and decided to nutmeg him.

It didn't work. The ball cannoned off Owen's shin, back past Dennis, but not quite as far as the penalty area. Owen was off like a whippet, leaving Dennis for dead. Madman rushed out and made himself big – but it was too late. Owen got there first, and as Madman despairingly spread himself, Owen fell away to unleash a rising right-foot drive that had "net-buster" written all over it.

Only in this case, a split-second after the ball whistled over the line, it burst something else first. Something unique, exquisite, priceless – *sacred* even. Something that, scaled-up in size, had once been Shot Down Over Libya. And now *this* smaller version had been Shot Down By The Liverpool.

Owen's blaster caught both the Gloster Gladiator's tailplane and the string it hung from. Off flew the model's back end, then down fell the whole of the rest of it. The impact was horrible. Both wings sheared off. The cockpit glass shattered. The fuselage splintered. The little brown-and-green heap now lying inside the goal looked less like a battle-plane than a bonfire about to be lit.

And Madman looked back at it.

What happened next became as famous, in its way, as the sight of Michael O scoring against Argentina. Every national newspaper the next day carried a still photo from the TV footage. And if Madman had been paid a pound for every time that bit of film was re-played up and down the country, he could have bought Roy Keane *and* had enough change to buy a cage to keep him in.

Owen just didn't know what hit him. He was getting to his feet when Madman, still on the deck himself, grabbed out at his ankles. His face had gone an Aston Villa shade of claret, with lips as white as a Leeds United home shirt. Luke heard him hiss *"You broke my plane!"* the first time. The second time, everyone in the stadium – and watching on TV – picked it up.

*"You Broke My Plaaaannnnnnnne!"*

As he'd shown so many times with his impressions, Madman could go way past ten on the dial when it came to volume. But what no one had known before was how strong he could be when roused. Still gripping Owen's ankles, he sprang up from the ground. The Reds' number ten came with him. Suddenly, as an eerie hush descended on both teams' fans, Madman was standing there with the Future Of English Football dangling upside down from his raised fists.

*"You Broke My Plaaaaaannnnnne!"*

Owen thrashed about a bit but Madman didn't even notice. All the players were too stunned to move in and sort it out. The ref blew his whistle to end the game, but he too stayed rooted to the spot. The only person in the whole gobsmacked stadium who moved was Madman himself. With Owen.

Slowly at first, then breaking into a jog, he headed for the tunnel. Owen waved his arms, and may have cried out the odd "Help! Help!" but any sound he made was drowned by Madman's ever-louder *You Broke My Plane*s. Luke looked on, as pop-eyed and helpless as everyone else. Those stocky little, upside-down legs in the red shorts were insured for thirty million *each*. And Madman really did look as if he might pull them off one by one – as though Owen was a spider he'd caught in the bath.

But as he came closer to the North Stand, he slowed down. And on the cinder track in front of the dug-outs, he stopped. Then Luke guessed what he actually had in mind. Holding his victim a little further away, Madman steadied himself – just like he did when he wound up to take a long-range goal kick. He was going to take a flying hack at England's Glory and boot him up into the crowd!

Every fan in front of him froze in horrified anticipation. This wasn't just mad, it was psychotic.

But then, in D stand, somebody moved. A hero! Out across the cinder track he dashed.

Luke watched agog as he swerved around a steward and lunged forward just as Madman's foot came back for the kick of a lifetime! So far back, in fact, that his boot-heel crunched sickeningly into the lunger's forehead.

Off flew a pair of Raybans as their owner hit the ground – knocked-out cold. Luke blinked. It was Neil Veal! He'd just *had* to save Morty from a moment of madness that would have wrecked his product-endorsement prospects for all time! And sure enough, after kicking Vealo, the keeper himself went spinning off balance until finally he tumbled to the ground and let Owen scamper free.

It was over. The whole petrified ground hummed back to life. It was as if everyone inside Ash Acre had just seen a member of the royal family escape an assassination attempt.

Madman didn't even see the ref red-card him as he began a long, broken-hearted trudge back to his busted plane. The TV viewers didn't see it either. Chrissie Pick had jumped in front of the camera, yanked up his Albion shirt and revealed the legend in biro beneath it:

**I LOVE MY HIAR!**

Few people spotted the spelling mistake. They were all still too traumatized.

At training on Wednesday morning no one said a word about Madman's rush of blood. Or *Krazy Keeper Tries To Kick Kop Kid*, as one tabloid headline put it. Craig told Luke that no one had mentioned it on Monday or Tuesday either.

Partly this was because no one knew quite what to say. But it was also partly because there were *other* things to talk about. Like the fact that after Sunday, the delighted directors had dug into their own pockets and paid the players two full weeks' wages. And like the fact that Albion were now through to the FA Cup semi-final: and their reward was a match on April the ninth at neutral Villa Park – against the Arsenal!

"But is Madman going to be able to play?" Luke asked Terry V, pulling off his training bib as they left the pitch together. "That red card will keep him out for a couple of games, won't it?"

"And the rest," sighed Terry. "You've seen what a storm the media's whipping up. Normally you'd only get a two-match ban for a sending-off. But this is somethin' else. You can't muck about with the likes of Michael Owen. Not on TV. Apparently the lad himself don't bear no grudge – he's even offered to help Madman glue the plane back together. But the FA's setting up a special tribunal. Madman might get it *extra* hard 'cos of all the bad publicity. Oh *why* did he have to go and do it when everyone was watchin'? If it'd been a run-of-the-mill League game, no one would even have heard about it."

"And how's Madman been?" Luke asked in the tunnel. "He looked pretty sick out there in training."

"Sick's the word. Have you seen the size of him? Chrissie says he ain't stopped pie-ing it ever since Sunday. And I'll tell you why it's a *double* flippin' disaster: there's not gonna be any replays in these semi-finals. New FA ruling. So if it's still a draw after extra time, it'll go straight to pens. With Madman in goal, we'd cream it in a shoot-out. Now he's shot us *all* in the foot."

There was a peculiar atmosphere in the dressing room. It could have been caused by the stink of the multi-coloured concoction Madman was cramming into his mouth from a wrapper that said *Tacky's Takeaway Tacos*. But it was more than that. Luke guessed that if Madman hadn't been there, everyone would still have been looping the loop about Sunday's performance. As it was, any mention of Liverpool was bound to conjure up images of plane wreckage and upside-down strikers. So it was tongue-holding time all round.

"Before you take your bath, lads," said Benny in the doorway, "just a few words about the Barnet game on Saturday. We don't come off too well at their place as a rule, and we'll have to be prepared for a pretty physical tussle. But look – I'm not gonna bother with putting up a teamsheet. It's gotta be the same starting line-up as we had on Sunday. Right?"

"Um – wrong," murmured Luke, raising his hand and shivering in advance.

"What's that, son?" The look on Benny's face was a mixture of horror and disbelief – as if he had just been shown a computer print-out of everything Madman had eaten that year.

"Sorry, Boss," Luke said. "I didn't know till last night. But my mum's invited my god-parents over for the afternoon. There's no way I'll be able to get away. I'll be all right for Swansea the week after, though. I'm with my dad then."

Benny swallowed hard as this sank in. Everyone did. For a moment even Madman stopped chewing. "Stone me," Benny said in the end, "we're gonna be in a right spot now."

"Me too," replied Luke. "My godparents both work in a bank and they spend hours advising me where to invest my pocket money. They even used to give me tips on what to do with the 50p's I got from the tooth fairy."

"Bankers, eh?" piped up Half-Fat. "They're usually loaded. You couldn't ask them for a few bob for poor struggling Albion, could you?"

"Well, while we're on the subject of readies," sighed Benny, "I've got to tell you all that *Lampshades Plus* aren't looking too healthy. The firm's shipping money at the same rate as we are. It's just a question now of which one goes belly-up first: the club or the sponsors."

"But we must be making tons of dosh from this Cup-run," Narris protested. "Look at the crowd we had on Sunday. Then there's all the TV fees…"

Benny put up both hands as if in surrender. "Don't shoot the messenger," he cried. "This goes way back before my time. Loans the club took out and never paid back. Hundreds of thousands of quid. God knows what they spent it on – the ground's still a shambles, and I can't remember the last time we actually bought a player. But now all the people we borrowed from want their cash back. I'm telling you straight: if some Fairy Godfather don't come in and bail us out, we're gonna go down like a lead balloon – Cup-run or no Cup-run."

A dismal silence fell. Madman swallowed the last of his taco and burped. Every other head in the room nodded. For once in his life, he'd spoken for them all.

Luke's dad finished the third song of his set with a power-chord. The song was a nineties reworking, for electric guitar and drum-machine, of Simon and Garfunkel's classic sixties anthem, "The Sound of Silence". Technically it didn't require a power-chord to round it off, Luke's dad just threw one in because, to him, it seemed right at the time. Sadly it didn't seem anywhere near as right to his guitar's D-string, which promptly snapped.

"Bit of a bummer, this," announced the guy who billed himself nowadays simply as Green. "But I've got another string out in the van. So rap among yourselves for a bit. I'm gonna have to take five."

"Thank Gawd for that," breathed Rocky Mitford, Chairman of the Castle Albion Supporters Club – and one of less than twenty paying punters scattered around the functions room of The Third Way pub. Then he realized Luke was sitting at the table right behind him. "No offence there, son," said the curly-haired Superfan, twisting around, "it's just not my sort of music, that's all."

"No offence taken," Luke smiled. He'd grown a skin as thick as a crocodile's where his dad's sixties songs were concerned. He loved the old boy right up to the end of his ponytail, but after all these years he seriously doubted that this was *anybody*'s sort of music. Did a world on the brink of the Millennium really *need* a bloke in a boozer "re-interpreting" "Happy Jack" by The Who on a banjo? Was there an irresistible demand for an instrumental version of The Move's "Blackberry Way" on unaccompanied bottleneck slide guitar?

As Green got up to leave the tiny stage he flashed Luke a wink and gave him a thumbs-up sign. To him at least – broken strings apart – this wasn't going at all badly. Three songs into the set, and there were still other people in the room. That had to count as a sort of result.

But the other people, it had to be said, had other reasons for being there. This was after all a charity gig for the football club's Fighting Fund. And everyone present was much more into "Come On You Albion" than a reggaed-up version of "Come And Get It" by Badfinger. All except Cool Frederick, that was. The elegant defender – frowning alongside Benny Webb at Luke's table, as Green tortured one song after another – knew more about music than Madman knew about pie fillings. He was also no mean vocalist himself – as he'd shown at the club's Karaoke Fundraiser a few weeks before.

"Maybe you ought to get up there and help him out a bit," Benny suggested.

"No way." Frederick shook his head. "His gig. 'Nuff respect."

"Well, it's good of him to give all the takings to the club," said Benny.

"Yeah, right," snorted Rocky, twisting round a second time. "Thanks to this, we'll be able to buy *really* big. D'you think we'll have enough for Darren Huckerby *and* Dwight Yorke?" He caught Luke's eye. "No offence again, son."

Benny shook his head sorrowfully. (He must have been sweltering inside his great sheepy coat but you never saw him out of it. It was like a second skin. According to Narris, it *was* his skin.) "If Elvis came back from the dead," he said, "and *he* did a gig for us, we still wouldn't raise all the cash we need. It's serious, lads. We're in real danger of folding before the end of the season."

"That'd be just like Albion, wouldn't it?" smiled Rocky, between gritted teeth. "Get all the way to Wembley – then go out of business before Cup Final Day!"

"Hang on," coughed Terry the physio. "First there's the little matter of beating the Arsenal."

He rolled his eyes. "I've really got me work cut out on that one."

"How d'you mean, Tel?" asked Benny. "Our injured list ain't too bad, is it?"

"Nah, I'm not talkin' about that. It's the venue that bothers me. Villa Park. I've never checked out the dressing rooms there before. I dunno *how* I'm gonna put the wind up them Arsenal boys before the game starts."

Benny nodded. "Just give it your best shot, Terry. We'll all appreciate whatever you can do." He sighed deeply. "Meanwhile, the quest for cash continues."

"Well, what about selling off a few of the club's assets?" said Rocky.

"You mean try to flog our players?" laughed Terry. "Who in their right mind would wanna touch any of our lot?" He glanced at Luke and Frederick. "Present company excluded, of course. And you two will only leave the club over my dead body. Yours as well – right, Boss?"

"Right," Benny agreed. "And we should be thinking about buying, not selling. If we can't get another keeper to stand in when Madman's suspended, Stuart Mann'll have to put on the gloves. Then *that*'ll leave us short in defence..."

"But how will you get a keeper to come here when you can't pay him any wages?" asked

Rocky, and everyone shook their heads. "And do we know yet when Madman's tribunal's gonna be?"

Benny looked at him solemnly. "They've fixed it up for next Wednesday morning. Lancaster Gate. I'll go with the lad. Try and stop him grossing out in the buffet car on the train. It's a rotten, stinking old business. I only hope he's on his game at Barnet on Saturday. We need three points there. *Bad*."

"*Bad*," echoed Terry.

"*Bad!*" Rocky spat, staring forlornly at the stage, where Luke's dad had now reappeared with his guitar re-strung and ready for more.

"Hey, thanks for your patience," grinned the happy hippy. "I think you'll find the wait worthwhile. This is a little thing I've just knocked into shape. It's still got a few rough edges but I know you're gonna love it." He strummed the scale of G and it sounded way out of tune. "The Beatles' version of 'Strawberry Fields Forever' had a backwards bit at the end of it. In a tribute now to its composer, the late great John Lennon, I'm gonna do the *whole song* back to front!" He smiled at the ceiling. "Hope you're listenin' up there, Johnny."

Rocky Mitford just stared into Luke's eyes. He didn't have to say a word.

"No offence taken," Luke assured him.

Lunch was late on Saturday. Lunch was *always* late on Saturday. So was lunch on Sunday. Luke's mum seemed to go into a time warp whenever she entered the kitchen. Some days she went in and never came out. No one quite knew where all the time went. But one thing was for sure: she didn't spend it following highly-complex recipes through to the last letter.

Her main standby meal nowadays was pizza and badly-burnt oven chips. Occasionally she would switch from oven to grill and dish up fishfingers – still with oven chips, although now that they'd been grilled they were even blacker at both ends. For special occasions – like this visit from Luke's godparents, Uncle Reginald and Aunt Ramona – she pushed the boat out and used both grill *and* oven. This led to a lot of smoke, a good deal more effing and blinding than usual, and a long-delayed presentation of dried-out mini-Kievs and bullet-hard jacket spuds. No one ate very much of it. Even Madman would have thought twice about sticking away the stuff on that table.

"I'm sorry," Luke's mum said with her cheesiest grin, when all the knives and forks had been gratefully laid to rest. "I didn't have time to make a pudding." She glanced at the clock on the dining-room mantelpiece. "But I'm sure our visitors can't wait to have a nice little chat with their godson – so why don't you three go on into the sitting room while Rodney washes up?" Her grin grew even cheesier. "And you won't be disturbed by any half-wit football fans going past on their way up to that dreadful stadium. There's no game there today."

"From what I've heard," boomed Uncle Reginald, "there might never be a game up there again. I've been told the whole club's on the point of bankruptcy."

Luke's mum looked as if she had just won the Lottery – and knocked back a tumbler full of her favourite cooking sherry in celebration. "Well, let's all keep our fingers crossed, shall we?"

"Oh yes, dear," piped up Rodney when she glared his way. Luke just looked down at the gruesome mess on his plate. He'd looked at the clock too. Two-fifty-eight. Two minutes to kick-off at Barnet.

"*Shall we, Luke?!*" his mum screeched.

"Yes mum," Luke muttered. "Anything you

say. Why don't we go and chat then, Uncle Reg and Aunt Ramona?"

It lasted for almost two hours. Luke wasn't stupid – in fact Benny often called him the smartest midfielder in Castle Albion's history – but he reckoned he understood less than a quarter of everything these people were telling him. They kept going on about his "portfolio" – which Luke had always thought was a town in South Wales. And when they suggested he should sell his (non-existent) shares in British Telecom and buy into Rio Tinto Zinc instead, he just smiled sweetly and said that he would give it some serious thought.

There was something about R and R that wasn't entirely human. But they *did* fuel themselves up in the normal human way. At one point, after Luke's mum had announced she was going for a lie-down, Aunt Ramona opened her bag and took out two brand new tubes of Pringles – one plain, one sour cream and onion. Obviously they'd learned not to rely on Luke's mum for food. While they ranted at Luke never to invest more than two per cent of his total capital value, they wolfed back the lot without letting Luke get a sniff. Then out came a six-pack of chocolate Swiss rolls and they set about bolting down three each.

But Luke wasn't really in the room with them at all. In spirit, he was there at Barnet's Underhill ground with Frederick, Benny and the rest. There were ten minutes left to play, and the score was still nil-nil.

He didn't need to be psychic to know this. Through the French doors to the dining room, he'd seen Rodney in his pink pinny making phone call after phone call, dialling up the *Castleline* – an 0891 number which gave a running commentary on each Albion game. Whenever Rodney put down the receiver, he made a nil-nil sign in front of his face with the thumb and first finger of both hands. The fourth time, Aunt Ramona spotted him and he had to pretend he was rubbing his eyes. Which wasn't all that convincing, since he still had his glasses on.

Luke's heart thumped. Nil-nil wasn't brilliant but a point was better than nothing. The night before, basement club Shrewsbury had stuffed Chester three-one. This brought them level on points with Albion, but still behind them in the table because they'd scored fewer goals over the season. If Albion now held out for the draw, at least that would give them a bit of extra breathing space.

Five minutes to go. Three minutes. One. Rodney made three more calls. Three times he made the zero-zero signal through the French doors. Come *on*, Albion! A point! The first League point they'd won in weeks! At last they were turning the corner. Then Rodney punched out the number one more time. Right away he stepped back, as if to avoid a ripe pineapple in flight. Then his face went fruit-coloured: first like plums, then nectarines, then a sickly banana-yellow.

"Excuse me," gasped Luke, jumping up from the sofa. "I've got to take a call."

"I didn't hear the phone ring," said Aunt Ramona through her last mouthful of chocolate Swiss roll.

Dashing through the doors, Luke snatched the receiver from Rodney's quivering hand. Surely it hadn't all gone pie-shaped again! For a moment he couldn't hear the frantic commentator's voice above all the din in the stadium and the lo-fi *Castleline*'s hiss and crackle. But then the awful news trickled through:

"...*And at the final whistle, with Albion undeservedly going down one-nil, I have to say that I've never seen anything like it! No! I tell a lie. I HAVE seen it done before – once, thirty years ago – by Leeds United's Welsh goalie Gary Sprake. Just like Madman Mort in the last minute of today's game, Sprake took aim to throw the ball out, held on to it for too long, and ended up hurling it hard into his own net!*" Luke closed his eyes in despair. "*What WAS Mort thinking of? He seemed to lose concentration at the vital moment, and now he's scored what must be regarded as the most bizarre own goal of the Nineties! What a week it's been for the Cock-eyed Keeper! Some of his highly-disappointed team-mates will probably be holding HIM upside down right now in the dressing room..."*

"Luke," barked his mum, appearing in the doorway. "Who are you talking to?"

"No one, Mum," Luke replied – which was honest enough – as he dejectedly replaced the receiver.

**13**

Since Benny was off with Madman at the tribunal, Terry took training on Wednesday. It wasn't a very impressive session. Terry Vaudeville reigned supreme as a loosener of doors and flooder of floors, but a football coach needs slightly different qualities from these and Luke soon realized that twinkle-eyed Terry was *way* short of them.

When he had the squad working on set-pieces, his directions were so confusing that Chrissie Pick ran full-pelt into a defensive wall and had to limp off. Then during the practice match, he made so many bad refereeing decisions that the usually ice-cool Gaffer Mann hurled the ball at him in disgust.

"Nice throw, Gaffer," said Half-Fat. "I wish Madman could have chucked it as accurately as that on Saturday."

"He *did* chuck it accurately," Dennis pointed out. "Right in his own flippin' net. All he cares about is that smashed-up plane of his and the tribunal."

"Oh, hark at him!" Narris snarled across at Dennis. "If *you* hadn't gifted that goal to Owen in the Liverpool game, there wouldn't *be* a smashed-up plane or a tribunal, *would* there?"

"Lads, lads," Terry clucked, rubbing the side of his head where Stuart's missile had hit him. "We're all a bit out of sorts and that's understandable, what with everythin' that's goin' on. But we can't let the pressure get to us – 'specially with this crunch game comin' up at Swansea on Saturday. So let's wrap it up for the morning, and all go inside and have a nice cuppa, eh?"

"That's the first sensible thing you've said all day," grunted Craig Edwards.

But even here, fate seemed to be against them. The players' tea-urn had been ripped off the wall, and a note had been sellotaped over the space: *Repossessed by order of the directors – due to lack of funds.* They'd taken the milk and sugar too, and both small packets of Chocolate Digestives.

"Where will it end?" Carl Davey groaned, fiddling with the pineapple he'd already bought for the Swansea trip. "They'll have us washing our own kit next."

"Ah," said Terry after a moment's silence. He'd gone the same shade of plum as Rodney on the *Castleline.* "As it happens, Benny *did* ask me to have a word with you boys about the laundry arrangements..."

In the uproar that followed, only Luke and Frederick noticed the dressing-room door open and Benny slouch inside. Misery was etched all over his face.

"Wha'appen, Boss?" asked Frederick, and suddenly everyone was silent.

"It could've gone better," said the ashen-faced supremo. Behind him in the doorway Luke could see Madman standing with his head bowed low. At first he couldn't work out why the Nutty One looked so weird. Then it hit him: for the first time in living memory, he wasn't in his keeper's kit. Instead he was wearing a suit – one that fitted him so tightly he must have bought it about two thousand pies and several hundred kebabs ago.

"So how many games is he out for?" Gaffer demanded. His temper hadn't cooled down much since taking his pot at Terry then finding the tea-urn gone.

"Well, as you know," Benny began, "any red card brings a statutory two match suspension. Morty got that – which means he's out for the next two games: Swansea away and Darlington at home. But then, in addition, they whacked on *another* two-match ban, for Bringing The Game Into Disrepute..."

"What're they *like!*" Narris groaned, kicking

the wall. "Football's *already* as disreputable as it gets. That's why everybody loves it!"

Benny chose to disregard that. "So now Madman's gonna have to miss the six-pointer at home against Shrewsbury..." He shuddered. "And also..."

"*THE FLIPPIN' CUP SEMI-FINAL AGAINST ARSENAL!*" every single player yelled, as their Wembley Dream began to fade before their eyes.

"'Fraid so," said Benny. Meanwhile Madman's head sank so low he seemed to be trying to inspect the contents of his own stomach from the inside. In his hand was the remains of a British Rail bacon sandwich that he just hadn't had the heart to finish off. "As you can imagine, Morty is ... well ... mortified."

"I'll mortify him!" roared Half-Fat, slumping on to the bench with his head in his hands. "That stupid prat's gone and wrecked it for us all."

"Why couldn't you just have behaved like someone *sane* for once in your life?" Craig wailed at Madman, whose lip was now trembling just like Gazza's before the floodgates opened at *Italia '90*.

"You're a disgrace!" Carl Davey screamed at him, apparently on the point of tears himself. "You're a big overgrown kid, and 'cos of you I'm never gonna get my chance to play where every player in the *world* wants to play!" Then he rocketed to his feet – his fingers pressed so hard into his pineapple that it looked more like a prickly orange bowling ball. "Why don't you clear off altogether! No one wants you here! *Go and play the fool at some other club!*"

And with that, he drew back his arm and sent the spoilt pineapple fizzing across the dressing room in the general direction of the doorway. Carl wasn't the Nationwide League's greatest marksman – with his foot *or* with his hand. The lump of fruit seemed to have Benny's name on it rather than Madman's. But the Boss saw it coming, ducked in time, and so it smashed noisily into a third -- unseen – person standing just outside.

"All right, Carl," quivered Madman. "You're right! I'm obviously not wanted here. Benny, I'm putting in a transfer request. As of now!" Then he turned on his heel and marched away – revealing to everyone a dazed-looking Neil Veal with pineapple chunks in his heavily-gelled hair and all over his Raybans.

After a queasy smile at Luke, Frederick and Chrissie, he too turned, and rushed after his client. "Madman!" Luke heard him yell along the corridor. "We've got to talk! Major Career Move! Let's do pie-and-mash, burger and chips, spaghetti carbonara – and then fresh-cream apple turnovers from Sainsbury's!"

**14**

As the Albion coach pulled into Swansea it was sleeting down with rain. "I've never been down here when it wasn't like this," muttered Craig Edwards. "I really hate this place. It's like being in another country."

Luke glanced sideways at Frederick. Both boys felt up for the game but hardly anyone else seemed to be. Luke couldn't help thinking Benny had made a mistake in asking Madman to travel with them. OK, so he wanted to keep the suspended shot-stopper involved (and maybe even get him to rethink his transfer request). But his miserable mood wasn't doing a lot for team morale. Nor was the aroma of the Indian meal for four that he'd brought along for company.

No one else wanted much to do with him. He sat alone in the two front seats, staring out at the rain and the fist-shaking Welsh fans, incapable of even the faintest aeroplane noise. In an attempt to cheer him up, Benny had dug out the old latex skeleton-chest that the keeper used to wear under his jersey, and had occasionally flashed at oncoming forwards. Glumly Madman put it on, then spilled cold chicken tikka all down the ribs. The man was a shadow of his former self – mentally if not physically (because his waist was thickening quicker than an Inspector Morse plot).

The driver got lost in the narrow streets around the ground. He hadn't performed too brilliantly on the motorway either. That was the calibre of driver you got when your club could only afford bargain-basement coach firms.

"Why don't *you* take the wheel, Madman!" shouted Narris from the back. "You got nothin' else to do. Besides, you might be needing a new career soon."

"Oh, I dunno," Craig chipped in. "There's always his *transfer*. Have Villa put in an offer yet, Madman? Or are they waiting till Chelsea and Everton's bids are on the table – so they can see what they've got to beat?"

"There's always Scotland too," Half-Fat reminded everyone as the giggles and titters got louder. "Rangers, Celtic – they do like a dodgy foreign keeper up there."

"And what about the real foreign sides?" Chrissie Pick laughed. "You won't believe this, but our agent's put together a video of Madman's greatest saves and sent it out everywhere: Europe, Japan, Australia."

Dennis guffawed. "I didn't know they *made* tapes that short!"

At that, Madman jumped to his feet and swung round to face his hecklers: all tikka-streaked latex and furiously screwed-up face. "You lot can carry on as much as you like!" he roared, and for a moment Luke heard aircraft-engines revving. "I've still got a big future in this game. I know my strengths. I can work on my weaknesses. One day I'll play for my *country*!"

"Oh, really?" Carl Davey enquired above the din of disbelief. "And what country would that be? Cloud-cuckoo-land?"

"*All right that's enough!*" boomed Benny, as the driver at last worked out how to stop circling the ground. "Siddown Madman! And the rest of you – start focusing on the job in hand. We can't afford no slip-ups here."

But slip-ups there were – first of all from Luke.

As both teams ran on to Vetch Field, the rain was reaching monsoon level. Luke didn't even get to his own penalty box before he skidded over in his trainers. Three times in the first fifteen minutes he did the same thing. Luckily he was some distance from the ball whenever it happened, but Benny didn't look too chuffed in the dug-out.

He looked less chuffed still after half an hour. So did makeshift keeper Gaffer Mann. Gaffer wasn't a natural goalie but he was a good all-round athlete and he wasn't going to let anyone down – especially when so many others were fully capable of letting *themselves* down. And the culprit in question in the thirty-first minute was The Big Hair Boy.

When Swansea won a corner, Chrissie tracked back to mark the Swansea number eight. They jostled and nudged each other at the near post – just like you're supposed to do at all set-pieces – but as the ball flew in hard the number eight suddenly *ducked* instead of jumped. That caught Chrissie on the hop. Too late, he saw the ball rocketing towards his face – or rather, his hair.

Instinct took over, and up came his hand to protect the magnificent mop. *A hair-raising mistake*, the local football paper called it later that day. All of Swansea screamed for a pen. And got it. And from the way the Sneaky Swans on the pitch celebrated, they gave the impression that they'd planned out in advance how to put Chrissie on the spot.

Gaffer dived to his right when the penalty was struck. The taker aimed for his left. Badly. The ball whistled past the post. Still nil-nil. Which was also the score at half-time (when Benny threatened to take shears to Chrissie if that ever happened again) and it was *still* the score with eighty-nine minutes gone.

But there was time yet for one final slip-up. Swansea threw everyone forward for a last big assault. They were looking for a place in the play-offs, and a measly point at home wasn't much use to them. As their seventeenth corner arrived in the box, Gaffer took charge and punched the ball clear. Only Luke, Carl Davey and three Swansea defenders stood between the two penalty areas. Luke reacted quickest, darting left to fetch the ball, glancing up, and driving an inch-perfect pass between the white-shirts for Carl to run on to.

Carl saw it early, set off like a whippet, and before you could say John Hartson, he was bearing down on the Swansea goal with no one else close enough to challenge. But Carl didn't need a Swan to put him off his stroke. Remembering how Michael Owen had fallen away to make a better angle before belting the ball past Madman, he also tilted to the right – but too far. When he then tried to shoot, his legs just scissored on the slippery surface and he fell in a heap without even making contact with the ball.

Benny and Terry were waiting for him in the dressing room. As soon as Carl entered Terry hurled the "lucky" pineapple at his posterior, scoring a direct hit.

"You *prat*, Carl!" Benny yelled. "You could have *blown* it in from there."

"We still got a point!" the non-striking striker yelled back.

"Yeah, but Shrewsbury got three!" Benny shook his head forlornly as Carl turned away to rub his tingling backside. "We've just hit the bottom."

Luke saw the news in the paper before he left for school on Wednesday morning. As usual, his mum had torn out the *Daily Mail*'s football pages and flung them in the swing-bin before reading the rest of it. But when his mum was in the loo, Luke noticed the small headline as he scraped the black bits off his toast: *Phiz To Pop Across Atlantic*.

Luke's heart plummeted as he read on. Thanks to an injury crisis, Trinidad had called up Narris at the last minute for a World Cup qualifier against Honduras. It was a great honour for him, of course. But it meant Albion would be without their midfield linchpin not only against Darlington at home that night, but also in the titanic relegation battle against Shrewsbury in three days' time. "This is terrible," he murmured to Rodney, who was reading it over his shoulder. "What are we going to do on Saturday?"

"I'll *tell* you what we're going to do on Saturday!" announced his mum, surprising them both by waltzing into the kitchen. Luke swung the bin shut and turned to find her smiling a mad tight-lipped smile, like someone who had just swallowed a whole set of teeth – not necessarily her own.

"Since it's your birthday next week," she declared, "I'm throwing you a party – this Saturday!"

"Er ... Mum," said a stunned Luke, noticing that Rodney was just as taken aback. "That's very kind of you. But really, I don't *need* a party..."

She wasn't listening. "It's going to be a *garden* party. Everyone must come dressed as a shrub or plant, or as an item of garden furniture. I've sent out all the invitations. And I've had replies from almost everyone already."

"From my friends?" asked Luke, baffled.

"From people *I* think it would be nice for you to be friendly with. Don't you worry – there'll be plenty of good company. You'll have a whale of a time."

Out she marched and Luke closed his eyes to picture it. Here, on Saturday afternoon – while the Albion took on Shrewsbury without Madman, without Narris and now without him too – *he* would be sitting in fancy dress with a gruesome array of cousins and neighbours' kids, tucking into his mum's horribly runny "jelly" and welterweight "fairy cakes".

He shuddered – and so did Benny Webb, later that morning, when Luke dropped his bombshell after training. "When are we gonna get a break?" Benny asked the dressing-room wall. "What have we done to deserve all this?"

"There's absolutely no chance she'll postpone it?" Terry asked.

"No chance at all," Luke told him. "When her mind's set on something, it's set." Unlike her jellies, he thought.

"Can't we postpone the game then, Boss?" Chrissie Pick suggested. "Clubs do that, don't they? When their squad's been depleted by international call-ups."

"But *we*'ve only got one bloke on international duty," Gaffer Mann wearily pointed out. "Does the FA shift fixtures 'cos of kids' birthday parties?"

Benny shook his head. "Postponements," he said. "There could be a ray of light there. You know them games of ours that got snowed off in January? Well, we'd re-scheduled a couple of 'em for April, but I'm trying to bring one forward again now. Like to next week." No one seemed sure what he was getting at. "Well *think* about it!" he almost snarled; all this pressure was really getting to him. "If we can slot in another League fixture between now and the semi-final, Madman will be able to play against Arsenal – *right?*"

"So what?" asked Craig. "Gaffer kept a clean sheet on Saturday. I reckon he played better than Madman usually does too."

"But we didn't have Gaffer on the *pitch* then, did we! And Arsenal are gonna have a bit more up front than Swansea – so are Darlington tonight – so we'll need the skipper to tie down Bergkamp and Anelka, won't we?" He lowered his voice. "But look, quite apart from that, you lot have *got* to go easy on Madman. Keep his pecker up. Help his self-image a bit, you know?"

"His *self-image*!" hissed Half-Fat. "And why are we whispering?"

" 'Cos he's probably out there in the corridor with that blessed agent of his," Benny explained. "Plottin' a move to some other club. I only wish I could think of a way to make the lad feel properly *wanted* during his lay-off."

"Well maybe you could pay him some wages," grunted Dennis. "Maybe you could pay us *all*..."

Luke headed smartly for the door, with Frederick close behind. Neither boy liked being around when the money stuff came up. And it kept on coming up. Regularly. "See you tonight," Luke called back with a wave to everyone.

Out in the corridor, Madman and Veal stepped back at once from the wall where they'd been pressing their ears. "They're all one hundred per cent behind you really," Luke told the goalie. "They'd hate it if you left the club. You know that."

"Well soon they might have to lump it," Madman snorted. "Neil here's been getting a few results from that video he put together."

"From other English clubs?" Luke wondered what video they could've sent out.

"Not as such," Veal intervened. "From a *little* further afield."

"France? Italy? Where?"

"Well, as it happens: Laos, Paraguay and Basutoland."

"Lesotho," murmured Cool Frederick.

"Bless you," grinned Veal, thinking he'd sneezed.

"No," added Luke. They'd done this in geography. "Basutoland's called Lesotho now. It has been for yonks. Maybe you should get a new atlas?"

Veal just grinned, as shameless as ever. "And maybe you and I should talk sometime? Let's do..." he cocked his head at the dressing-room wall, through which he'd so recently been eavesdropping, "...party tea?"

**16**

Luke got to Ash Acre in good time for the Darlington game. He'd told his mum there was a "Maths Sleepover" for five boys in his class – at Cool Frederick's house. She hadn't looked convinced at first. Then Rodney had volunteered to keep driving over for spot-checks. This put her mind at rest – and also enabled Rodney to nip in and out of Ash Acre during the clash with the League leaders.

More people than usual were milling around outside the ground. Most of them were kids. "Desperate attempt to get bums on seats," explained the doorman at the players' entrance. "Or – in the case of the South Side – bums on terraces. Anyone under the age of ten gets in free tonight. But the kids bring their dads and *they*'ve got to pay." He pointed down a corridor at someone being fitted into a giant cross-eyed lion outfit – complete with a bushy nylon mane and an outsized Albion shirt. "They've got *him* out of mothballs too."

"Why!" grinned Luke. "It's Kingsley Castle. Good to see him back."

Kingsley had first appeared two seasons before in one of the club's botched attempts to lure in more fans. All he had to do was wander around inside the ground before kick-off, shaking kids' hands and posing for photos with them. Unfortunately the man within – a local unemployed actor – got stage-fright at his third game, did a runner, and could never be tempted back. And since the outfit was his own, and he wouldn't let anyone else wear it, that was the end of KC – till now.

There were some less familiar faces in the dressing room: five lads from the now-defunct youth team – three to sit on the bench and two to fill the outfield holes left by Narris and Gaffer. They all looked as frazzled as Kingsley Castle just before he went AWOL. What a way to make your debut, though – dragged into the League's bottom team against the slick northern table-toppers!

When the moment came, instead of giving a tactical talk, Benny handed round handwritten exercise-book pages. Every one of them was different. "What's this, Boss?" asked Dennis. "Diet sheets?"

"No, son. They're run-downs on the players you're each likely to come up against: strengths, weaknesses, tricks to watch out for, ways to wind them up. I had both our next opponents – Darlington and Shrewsbury – watched last week. The scouts sent me detailed reports. Then I wrote up them sheets."

Luke glanced at his own. All it said was: *Let them worry about you, lad. Just play your own game.* Looking sideways, he saw that Cool F's said the same.

"You can turn Villa over. You can beat Newcastle and Wolves. You can *thrash* Liverpool," Benny said before opening the door to let them out. "There's no reason on earth why you can't get a result against Darlington. *Do it!*"

The atmosphere under the lights was weird. Perhaps it was the sound of a thousand squealing free-entry kids – though the noise they made when Kingsley Castle played keepy-uppy with a balloon was much louder than their cheering for the Albion. Not that they *had* much to cheer about.

Everyone except Luke and Fred – and Gaffer in goal – seemed slightly bamboozled by the opposition. Several times Luke saw Carl or Half-Fat or Craig scratch their heads in puzzlement after a passage of play. Twice Chrissie tried to drift inside his full-back – which he *never* usually did – and ran into a covering defender both times. Even Ruel kept trying to turn his marker to the left when usually he spun away to the right, and kept on losing the ball. Benny was making frantic hand-signals from the cinder track but, as ever, no one on the pitch could make head or tail of them.

All this started to matter less on the stroke of half-time. Gaffer rushed out of his area to break up a Darlington attack. Comfortable on the ball, he didn't just hoof it into touch. Luke was free in the centre-circle and asked for it to feet. Gaffer obliged. As he turned, Luke noticed Frederick accelerate past him – into Carl Davey's usual attacking channel. No one picked him up, so Luke pinged a pass straight into his path – putting just enough backspin on the ball to make it sit up for Cool F's half-volley from thirty-five yards out.

*Oh my word!* If the Darlington keeper had hung a plane from his right-hand stanchion, it would now have been flying above the Town End – in a million tiny pieces. The away fans behind the goal were just relieved that the net saved them from instant decapitation. Castle Albion one Darlington nil! The home team were still high-fiving Frederick as they all burst into the dressing room at half-time.

"Stonkin' goal, Frederick," nodded Benny. "Lovely move to make it, Gaffer and Luke. But look lads, I've got to come clean on this one –

those sheets I gave you: they was for the Shrewsbury game..."

Everyone groaned as the penny dropped. "So is that why everything on here was wrong?" asked Carl, holding up his sheet and flipping it.

"Not wrong," Terry replied, rescuing his Boss. "Just no use *today*. This Darlo lot are pretty cute though, eh? Even brought their own generator. It's as if they'd *guessed* I was gonna fuse the lights." He sighed. "Which, in all fairness, I was. But they're not really on it tonight, are they? I reckon we'll 'ave 'em."

"You're already halfway there, lads," cried Benny as they trooped out again a few minutes later. "Remember Liverpool!"

And they did remember the Liverpool game – in the way they stroked the ball around all second-half, the way they made high-flying Darlo look second-best in all areas, the way they felt that they just couldn't lose. But as injury time loomed, they remembered the Liverpool game for another reason. Because that was when the visitors snatched a late goal – and this time a share of the points too.

It wasn't anyone's fault. No one, from Gaffer through to Ruel, made a blunder. Sometimes in football you just have to hold up your hands and salute pure class. Which was what Darlington's spunky number four had in spades as he broke from midfield, dummied a pass to his right, feinted left, then rifled a fearsome low drive across Gaffer and into the far corner. The shabby old ground echoed to a chorus of high-pitched wails of despair.

Benny and Terry were waiting po-faced in the dressing room. Everyone's head was so low as they trooped in that for a while no one saw the third "person" present. "Hey!" said Carl, the first to notice, "What's *he* doing in here?"

Luke turned with the others to find a very droopy cross-eyed lion up on the physio's bench. He'd never seen such a fraught-looking pantomime animal. Was he having another nervous breakdown after only one match back?

"I just wanted to keep him involved," mumbled Benny. "Take your head off, son." Off it came with a tug on the mane – to reveal underneath an utterly dejected Madman Mort. "And I wish I could take *my* head off," Benny went on. "It hurts, lads. A lot. Shrewsbury have won again. We're gettin' left behind."

**17**

"*Rodney!*" Luke's mum screeched. "Your Mr Mallard is on the phone! Does he have to ring up *every* Thursday evening? I've got better things to do than keep taking calls from him!"

Up in his room, Luke went rigid. There was no Mr Mallard. It was a code-name Rodney used for Benny Webb. And he usually rang on a Thursday, just to check that Luke was going to be all right for the following Saturday. But this Saturday was a non-starter, as Benny well knew. Luke could hardly bunk off from his own birthday party. So what on earth did Benny want now?

He didn't find out for quite a while. His mum had sniffed something suspicious in the air (other than the cakes she was baking for Saturday). For the rest of that evening she wouldn't leave Rodney alone in a room with Luke. Luke's stepdad even tried to creep along to his bedroom in the middle of the night – but his mum also chose just that moment to "need the bathroom".

They finally got their chance to chat at breakfast the next morning – when the postman arrived with a massive parcel that Luke's mum had to sign for. She was out of earshot for only two minutes but that was long enough for Rodney. Just.

"It's Halifax," he whispered across the table.

"*What*'s Halifax?"

"Next Monday night. They've agreed to bring the re-arranged fixture forward. It'll mean Madman can play against Arsenal. But Benny was ringing to see if *you* could play. Against Halifax. On Monday."

"Monday?" Luke whispered back. "That's my birthday..."

"Right! So I suggested Benny should ring your dad. *He'll* be ringing your mum any minute. To ask if he can have you that night – to give you a birthday treat."

"Hold on, though," hissed Luke. "Halifax – that's not very near here, is it? If I'm going to get there in time, I'll need the afternoon off school as well."

"Benny's already squared that with your headmistress." He grinned. "Good job she's so keen on football."

"Keen on *what*?" Luke's mum gasped from out in the hall. "Did I hear someone in there using obscene language?" But she didn't sound quite as homicidal as usual. She must have been pleased to get her parcel – which Luke and Rodney could now hear her ripping into. Moments later, the phone rang.

"Ah, hello," said Rodney after reaching for the kitchen wall-phone. "What a pleasant surprise to hear from you... Yes, all right then... Yes, I'll just give her a shout." He put the receiver to his pink-pinnied chest. "It's for you, dear," he called out, eyeing Luke nervously and crossing the fingers of his free hand. "It's Luke's dad. He wants to make an arrangement for Monday evening."

"I can't come now!" The sound of cardboard tearing had given way to loud bubblewrap rustling. "What *about* Monday evening? That's Luke's birthday."

"Yes, dear. That's what he was wondering. Whether he could meet Luke from school and take him out for a treat?"

Briefly the rustling stopped. Luke could almost feel Rodney's toes curling up inside his shoes as the tension mounted. Then to his great surprise, after more rustling out in the hall, he saw his mum's dressing gown go sailing past the kitchen doorway, followed closely by her pyjamas. Tops *and* bottoms. What was she up to out there? Had the parcel been a self-help book on stripping?

"So will that be all right then, dear," Rodney pressed on, up on tiptoe now from the strain.

"He'll pick him up from school and have him for the night?"

Another pause. Longer than the first. "I don't think that's very fair," the invisible woman said at last. "In that case I'd hardly get to see Luke on his birthday. And his dad's already having him *tomorrow* night. But because Monday's a special day, I'll be generous..." Luke and Rodney raised their fists in a huge, silent *Yessss!* "...Luke must come home here after school, then his dad can come and pick him up at – oh, what shall we say? – eight o'clock?"

Both fists fell. Eight o'clock. The game in Halifax would already have kicked off. Luke could forget about playing. "Um..." Rodney bravely panted, "Well he *was* wondering if he could have him a bit earlier. You see..."

*"I have given my reply! I refuse to negotiate any further! DO YOU UNDERSTAND ME?!"*

Luke's mum liked to make her position clear on these things. Then she liked everyone else to take up exactly the same position as herself. *Or else*.

Quickly Rodney explained the situation to Luke's dad then sadly replaced the phone. Luke did not have time even to meet his eye before his mum reappeared in the kitchen doorway – wearing a dazzlingly manic grin and, thankfully, something else as well. But what *did* she have on?

"Whaddaya think?" she demanded of the two men in her life, pressing both arms close to her sides to give them the full effect.

"Um... Ah... *Splendid!*" Rodney managed to spit out. "It's really ... *you.*"

Luke was just too gobsmacked to speak. Was this what they meant when they talked about women having a mid-life crisis? She had dressed herself up to look exactly like a bird-table made of distressed pine, complete with a little house around her head, and nuts on strings hanging down from her fringe.

"It's for the *garden party!*" she explained, obviously miffed that they thought she'd ordered it for everyday use. "Fancy dress – *remember!*" Her look darkened. "Now come and see what *you're* both going to be wearing."

**18**

Luke's dad took him out for a burger on Friday evening. It was still quite early when they finished eating, so Green Senior suggested calling round at Frederick's place on the way home. "A couple of weeks back I asked him to track me down a record," he said in the van. "An original vinyl copy of the Electric Prunes' first album. Let's give him a buzz and see if he's scored."

There were no lights on at Cool F's house, but that didn't mean much. Only Frederick's sister lived in there. The lad himself had a little self-contained pad in the back garden. That was where he kept his awesome library of records, CDs and cassettes. When Luke's dad got in there, he was as happy as George Best let loose in a roomful of Miss Worlds.

"I'm sorry," Frederick's sister Adele said over the intercom, after Luke had pressed the bell, "Frederick's just gone out. He's taken another batch of singles up to that young guy's house on the hill, you know?"

Luke did know. Weeks before, computer whizzkid James Prince, founder of Majestic Software, had contracted Cool F to search out for him a complete collection of Eurovision Song Contest winners. Luke had gone with Frederick up to the mansion to deliver one set of records, but Prince's heavies hadn't let them past the front gates. Which was a shame. Luke had really wanted to have a nose around the home of a super-rich super-nerd, and he wondered if Frederick had actually made it inside this time.

"Is there a message?" Adele asked.

"No – not really," Luke answered. "Just wish him luck against Shrewsbury tomorrow. Bang one in for me, tell him."

"And say I'll be coming by at around noon on Monday," Green put in. "The dude can bring as many tapes as he likes. It's a long road to Halifax!"

"*You*'re going to Halifax?" Luke said on the way back to the van.

"Special request from the Boss," his dad smiled. "The club can't afford to charter a coach, so he asked me if I'd rock on up there anyway, even though you can't play. I'm taking Frederick, Half-Fat and another guy yet to be decided. I'm cool with that. We've all gotta pull together, right?"

"Right." Luke clicked himself into his seatbelt. His dad had clean forgotten he was meant to be having Luke from eight o'clock onwards on Monday evening. His memory wasn't great. The rock'n'roll lifestyle and everything. Luke would cover for him, though: tell his mum a last-minute gig had come up. But that wasn't his main concern. His dad was going to be taking three footballers to a crucial fixture several hundred miles away – and he was by no means the world's smoothest driver. By the time they got to Yorkshire, the poor saps would hardly be able to stand, let alone play football.

In fact, by the time the multi-coloured van jerked to the end of Cool Frederick's street, Luke himself was already beginning to feel the worse for wear. Then, as they turned into the main road, he spotted two faces he knew coming out of the chip shop. His dad saw them too and juddered the van to a sickening halt.

"Hey!" he cried, unbelting and leaping out. "Chrissie! Madman!" Luke got out too, once he'd resettled his stomach.

"Hi there, Mr Green," piped Chrissie. "All right then, Studless?"

Madman, eerily quiet, just nodded at the Greens. Then he dipped into the biggest bag of ocean sticks Luke had ever seen, pulled one out and started to suck on it thoughtfully. This was *weird*. Now that he was eligible for the Arsenal semi-final, Madman should have been like a pig in clover. At the very least, Luke had expected a Tornado GR1 impression up and down this row of shops – with or without its payload of Paveway laser-guided bombs.

"Hey, Madman," Luke said. "Great news about the Arsenal game, eh?"

"Yes and no," Madman replied after – rather reluctantly – removing the stick.

"How d'you mean?"

He reached into the back pocket of his tracksuit bottoms. But instead of producing something else to eat, he found a letter and handed it to Luke. There wasn't a street-lamp near by and it was hard to make out the words. It didn't help that the letterhead was all in a foreign language.

"He's been called up for a World Cup qualifier," Chrissie explained, popping a chip into his mouth then patting the side of his hair with greasy fingertips.

"But for what country?" Luke's dad asked, peering over his son's shoulder. "What does that say? *Waldovia?*"

"It's one of them new countries in eastern Europe," Chrissie went on, as if *everyone* knew that. "There's loads of 'em. You know – Estonia, Latvia, Belarus, Macedonia ... and Waldovia."

"But how come they've picked you, Madman? Are you ... Waldovian?"

He shook his head. "Only a bit. My grandad

was from out there though. I dunno what they used to call it in his day. But now it's Waldovia – and I've got enough Waldovian blood in me to qualify."

"They got on to him after seeing that video old Vealy sent," added Chrissie, who seemed more worked up about this than Madman. "It's amazing, he can get *him* an international call-up, and can't even get *me* a Wash & Go advert!"

Luke read on. "So the game's against the Ukraine. Blimey – they're good! And it's on—"

"April the tenth," nodded Madman. "The same day as the Arsenal game."

Luke gasped then handed back the letter. "So what'll you do?"

"What *can* I do?" This was a totally different Madman. Soft-spoken, wistful smile – he almost looked grown-up. "It's the classic problem, isn't it? Club versus country. I'd *like* to play in a Cup semi-final, but then again, it's the ultimate honour to represent your country. I'll have to consider it very carefully."

*Consider?* thought Luke as he got back in the van after saying goodbye to the lads. *Carefully?* Maybe Madman *had* gone for that NHS brain transplant?

**19**

Luke's mum had scheduled the party to start at four o'clock. But Luke started getting into his kit an hour before that – at precisely the moment when, just up the road, Albion were kicking off against comrades-in-peril Shrewsbury.

The outfit was a complicated, fragile thing made out of polythene and white-painted balsa-wood. Why on earth anyone would want to impersonate a greenhouse was a question Luke couldn't answer. How much his mum had *paid* for it, he didn't even like to think about.

After slotting together the last two bits of frame, he stood in front of the mirror and prayed – hard – that no one he respected would ever see him this way. He looked like an astronaut in a see-through spacesuit. And how he wished it hadn't been transparent! Underneath, he was wearing a tight white dancer's leotard with bright red tomatoes painted all over it. This was *not* flattering.

But at least while he changed, he'd been able

to have his radio on – stuffed under the pillow to muffle the sound. He didn't, after all, want his mum to catch him listening to the first-half commentary of Albion v the Shrews.

It was a weird experience. From Luke's bed came a kick-by-kick account of the action. Meanwhile through the window wafted the cheers and groans of the crowd as they responded. More groans than cheers, it had to be said.

There were no goals, but the radio guy was in raptures about Cool Frederick's performance. Time after time he tidied up when someone else went missing in defence. And *three times* Mighty Mr Dulac got forward himself and struck the Shrewsbury woodwork with powerful headers. Hence the groans.

"Come *on*, Albion," Luke murmured, closing his eyes on his own absurd reflection and – as the crowd's noise suddenly swelled – feeling as if he was actually *there* on the South Side, catching his breath at yet another effortless Cool F tackle. "When he moves forward," purred the commentator, "it's as if the ball is attached to his boot by a satin ribbon..." Yes, Luke could see that.

"He glides into the Shrewsbury half..." Luke saw those elegant, long strides. "Davey makes a good run to his left but Dulac veers sharp right, past two defenders..." Luke could see them lose balance! The crowd all around him was roaring Cool F on. "...Bibbo moves towards the penalty spot, screaming for the ball..." *Yes!* They'd worked on this in training. It was a decoy run by Ruel while behind him Half-Fat would be zeroing in on the far post. "...Dulac ignores Bibbo, looks up, threads a tantalizing ground-pass to the far post..."

The torrent of noise through the bedroom window then told Luke all he needed to know. "...Where Michael 'Half-Fat' Milkes arrives to blast the ball first time high into the roof of the Shrewsbury net!"

"Yes! Yes! Yes!" Luke whispered through gritted teeth and punched the air.

Just then his door opened. "What *are* you up to?" asked a rather stroppy-looking bird-table. "And what's that noise coming from your bed?"

"Oh nothing, mum." Luke dived across to flick the radio dial around to some posh-sounding piano music. "Just lost the signal for a minute."

She narrowed her eyes. The sounds of celebration from Ash Acre were still seeping through the window. "Come down," she said. "Your first guest's here."

This first guest – the son of the garden centre's manager – came dressed as a sunflower. For a present he'd brought Luke a packet of tulip bulbs. The second arrival was the girl of seven from two doors down. She *also* came as a sunflower, promptly burst into tears, then sulked for the next two hours. Luke hardly knew the remaining half-dozen guests. But every single parent who dropped them off took one look at him and said "Don't throw stones!" "Sorry?" he had to keep asking. " 'Cos you live in a glass house! *Geddit?*"

Luke got it all right. So did poor old Rodney. No man of forty should have to walk around his own home dressed as a gro-bag, with little green shoots sprouting out of his chest. But that was the outfit Luke's mum had got him, so that's what he had to wear. And it was his job to organize the first game: Pass The Parsley.

Fifteen deadly minutes later, Luke's mum clapped her hands. "Right! Everyone outside. Front garden – it's too muddy at the back. It's time for Clip The Leaves Off The Hedge!"

As soon as they left the house Luke heard the Albion crowd again: singing. (And since in their case they *did* only sing when they were winning, they still had to be one goal to the good!) Luke's mum scowled up the hill at the floodlights. For a split second Luke could have sworn he saw the pylons flinch. Then something worse happened. The singing stopped. No, not all the singing. *One* tiny little pocket of voices in the ground was now singing. Fit to burst.

Luke's legs almost gave way in their polythene and balsa-wood trousers. He knew that sound. His mum was explaining how each child had to be blindfolded, spun round, then he or she had to try to cut a leaf off the holly hedge with some blunt-looking shears. Luke barely listened. All he could hear was the singing. About two hundred voices, he reckoned. Two hundred voices that spoke – and sang – with a Shropshire accent. Shrewsbury were level!

"No, no, *no*!" his mum roared at his cousin Duncan (a horrible boy that everyone called "Donuts"). He'd wandered into the street and was doing his best to cut a lamp-post in two. "Get that blindfold off. Next contestant!"

Up stepped Little Miss Sulky Sunflower. But Luke wasn't watching. Just a bit further down the street he'd seen a familiar silver-grey BMW. *Agent Veal alert!* After that equalizing goal, Luke's heart hardly had any further to sink. Yet down it went again now. *Let's do party tea*, Veal had smirked on the day when he'd been listening in at the dressing-room door. And he'd meant it! The guy was phenomenal. He still believed that if only he could catch Luke's mum in a good mood, she would *gladly* sign the forms to put her son in his clutches.

But where was he hiding? Luke cast his eyes around, but sign of the agent was there none. Still it was deathly silent up at Ash Acre – apart from that couple of hundred full-throttlers. Come *on* Albion! Luke prayed, closing his eyes for extra force. You *can't* drop two more points.

But they did. Three blasts on the whistle sounded – faint but final. It was all over. This had been a true six-pointer and Albion had wound up with one. As if to express the pain Luke felt, a howl rose up from the corner of the front garden. Followed by another. Then another. Each one louder than the last.

Luke's mouth fell open. So *that* was where Neil Veal was. Surprised by all the kids (and Luke's mum) coming out, he'd wedged himself into the holly hedge wearing a bottle-green frogman's suit that blended perfectly with the colour of the leaves. But now that Blindfolded Miss Sunflower was pumping the shears open and shut on his right knee, he couldn't seem to get himself out again.

"OK, OK," cried the Gro-bag, rushing to pull off the girl before Luke's mum could identify Neil V. "Get all the kids back inside, dear. I'll deal with *him*!"

And for once – profoundly puzzled – she did just as he asked her. As Luke trudged back down the drive with the others, he looked over his shoulder to see Rodney helping Veal out of the herbaceous border. "Are you *mad*?" he heard his stepdad ask before pointing him back out to his car. A fair question.

"Hey, nice rescue," the agent breathed as he limped away. "We should talk about Luke, you and I." He patted a lump in the thigh of his frogman suit which had to be a folded-up client contract. "Let's do..." he paused, "...sunflower seeds?"

**20**

Luke wasn't really looking forward to his birthday. How could he? He should have been in Halifax – with people who really needed him. But as it turned out, he had a pretty good day.

His first surprise came straight after school. His mum came to pick him up as usual – but there in the back of the Escort were two people he was *always* pleased to see. His nan and grandpa from up in Doncaster.

"Aye, we couldn't let your birthday pass without giving you a right good Yorkshire greeting," beamed his grandpa. "Put it there!" He reached forward and grabbed his grandson's hand. Luke gasped as his fingers went into the vice. It was a good job he didn't have any homework that night. After a "greeting" from his grandpa – the Vinnie Jones of handshaking – he couldn't hold a pen for hours.

"We thought we'd take you ten-pin bowling, lad," said his nan as they drove off. "Rodney's going to meet us at the alley. But first we'll feed you up. You look as if you could do with a good blow-out." It was true. His mum had been serving up party leftovers since Saturday. And when you didn't fancy the sooty sausages-on-sticks the first time round, they didn't look any more appetizing in your lunch box two days later.

Luke pigged out at Harry Ramsden's, then the four of them strolled across to the leisure centre where Rodney was locking up his bike and struggling to get out of his cycling helmet. "Here, let me help!" cried Grandpa, tugging so hard at the strap that he got the helmet off but almost executed his son-in-law.

They bowled for three hours. When these old folks decided to do something, they liked to do it properly. Unlike their daughter. After just half an hour she said the fluorescent lighting was giving her a migraine and she had to go and sit in a dark place. This turned out to be the neighbouring five-screen cinema complex, where *The Lawnmower Man* was showing. Halfway through, she reappeared with a face like thunder. "It had *nothing* to do with gardening!" she stormed. "And now my head's feeling worse than ever. If you insist on playing this ridiculous game all night, I'm going home. Rodney, drive me! *Now!*"

She threw the car keys at him and stalked out. Rodney was gone for twenty minutes.

When he got back, the four of them had the tightest, most nail-biting all-against-all match Luke had ever played in. Grandpa led from the first round right the way through to the last but one. Then with his fourth strike of the night, Luke eased just ahead of him. As he turned to receive sportsmanlike applause from his nan and stepdad, Grandpa simply came up and put out his hand. "Lovely shot, lad," he said. "Put it there."

Luke tried to spring away but too late. Back in the vice went his fingers. They were so numb after that, he could hardly pick up the ball for his last throw – which dribbled down the side without hitting a single skittle. Grandpa meanwhile got six and that was enough to make him the winner.

"By heck, lad," he grinned, hugging Luke in consolation. "The old ones are the best ones! But it was the wrong sort of game for you, wasn't it? I know you'd much rather have been up in Halifax tonight. We heard all about it from your dad. But never you mind. We've fixed it with your mum for you to come to us this weekend. Birthday treat." His eyes twinkled. "We're taking you on an outing to Villa Park. Albion v Arsenal. You'll like that, now won't you?"

"Oh, brill, Grandpa!" Luke grinned. "I've *got* to play in that one!"

"I wonder how Albion are doing now?" asked Nan, glancing at her watch.

It was a question Luke had asked himself roughly five thousand times over the past hour and a half. "They'll be nearly finished now," he said, glum again.

Nan put her arm round him. "It's a right shame you couldn't play, lad, but there we are. Now... All that bowling must have got you hungry again. How about a little snack on the way home? What d'you fancy?"

"Spring rolls and king prawns!" said Luke in a flash. It was his birthday, for heaven's sake! And he needed more real food before going back on the Dodgy Sausage Diet in the morning. "There's a Chinese takeaway by the cinema."

The bloke behind the counter got all worked up when Luke's group came in. Instead of taking their order, he jumped about pointing at the overhead TV set. "Well blow me, lad," Grandpa smiled up at the screen. "It's *your* lot, Luke."

And it was. The local ITV news were doing a little preview of Sunday's Albion-Arsenal clash at Villa Park. In a quickfire ten-second section, they showed Albion banging in Cup goals against Villa, Wolves, Newcastle and Liverpool. When Luke's chip tied David James in knots, the other customers all clapped.

"Turn up the sound then," said Grandpa. "Let's hear what they're saying."

"*But how is it,*" asked Gary Newbon over much more recent pictures of Carl, Dennis and Co labouring against far more modest opposition, "*that Albion can hit such high notes in the Cup yet barely manage a croak in the League?*"

"It's the Halifax game!" cried Rodney. "What happened? What *happened?*"

"*Here at the Shay tonight, it took a while for several of the Albion players to find their feet...*" A snatch of film showed both Cool Frederick and Half-Fat running around as if their legs were different lengths. Luke clapped a hand to his head. His dad had driven them up there – jerking and lurching all the way, flinging them about like balls in a Lottery machine. No wonder they looked as sick as parrots. (But he'd said he was taking *three* – so who was the third?) "*...yet they put up a stout defensive performance until the seventy-third minute, when...*" Luke shuddered as the next clip began well inside Albion's half. This was it. They were going to go one down. "*...a misunderstanding between stand-in keeper Stuart Mann and Craig Edwards led to this soft near-post goal.*"

As the ball crept over the line as apologetically as Luke's last throw at the bowling alley, the image on the screen suddenly gave way to Benny Webb's bearded face with a mike thrust in front of it. It was his post-match interview by the dug-out. They weren't showing any more action! Albion had *lost*!

*"Not the ideal preparation for a Cup semi-final, Ben?"* asked Gary Newbon.

"No, Gary." Benny had shouted himself hoarse. You could hardly hear him.

*"Stuart Mann will be disappointed with the way that goal went in?"*

"Ah, you can't blame the Gaffer. He's done magic for us since Morty's been out. But Madman'll be back for the Arsenal game. Then we'll see. Cheers."

Benny turned to leave, but walked smack into an extremely groggy-looking cross-eyed lion. Benny soon righted himself and strode away with as much dignity as he could muster. But the lion continued to stagger about. And then it hit Luke: Mr Mort must've been his dad's other passenger.

But as the groans at Albion's deepening crisis began all round him, Luke wondered why Benny had been so sure Madman would be starting at Villa Park. What about the Waldovian call-up? Had he decided to put club before country?

At training the next morning, everyone found out.

**21**

When Luke arrived in the dressing room on Wednesday morning, Narris was getting all sorts of stick from the rest of the team. Trinidad had lost their World Cup qualifier and Narris had come on for only *five* minutes as sub.

"All the way to Trinidad just to get beat one-nil by Honduras!" Half-Fat was laughing. "You could have stayed here and got beat one-nil by Halifax!"

"Perhaps we wouldn't have lost if I'd been playing," Narris shot back.

"All the more reason not to put your country before your club," said Dennis.

"Put a sock in all that!" yelled Terry Vaudeville, bringing them to order. "Now we've got *another* little club v country question to sort out – right, Chrissie?" He gave the Big Hair Boy a broad wink, and several others tittered too.

"What is it?" asked Ruel, looking up from tying his boots. "What's the joke?"

Chrissie Pick tapped his nose at the veteran –

and at anyone else who now looked puzzled, including Luke. "Just wait and see. Any minute now."

As if on cue, the door swung inwards and Madman entered.

"What *have* you got on?" Carl snorted, throwing his hands over his face as if he'd been dazzled. It was easy to see why. Instead of his usual keeper's kit, Madman was rigged out in neon pink flares and a canary-yellow fleece, topped off by a bobble hat in Astroturf-green.

"These," Madman announced with a jutting jaw, "are the colours of my country. I had to search pretty hard – and pay well over the odds – to find clothes in the *exact* shades of pink, yellow and green. But as a true Waldovian, I feel that it's my duty to make that kind of effort."

"So does that mean it's your duty to *play* for your nation, as well?" asked Chrissie with a huge grin.

Madman raised his eyes and stared solemnly at the damp patch on the ceiling. "Lads," he said, "Benny, Terry – as some of you may be aware, I've recently been forced to make an agonizing decision about this Saturday. Do I play for Albion in the biggest game in *any* Third Division club's history? Or do I accept the game's ultimate honour and represent my family's homeland?" He sighed, still staring up – so he didn't see Chrissie, Craig and Half-Fat all bent double, trying not to explode with laughter. "I've thought long and hard about it, but now my decision is made." He placed a clenched fist over his heart. "*Laog ni Tarp Taf*," he said. "That is the motto of the Waldovian FA. I say it with pride. And on Saturday I will wear their national colours with pride as I do my international duty. Benny, Terry, everyone – I'm gutted to have to miss the Arsenal game. Really I am. But my people need me. I have to be with them."

At that point, the three players with their fists in their mouths couldn't hold back any longer. Half-Fat was laughing so hard, he fell off the bench on to the floor. Tears streamed down Craig's cheeks as he hooted and slapped the wall.

"What's up with you?" Madman asked, baffled. None of them could answer.

"*Waldovia?*" Cool Frederick then echoed. He'd obviously heard nothing about Madman's call-up before this. "You've been picked to play for ... *Waldovia?*"

"Yeah!" said Madman, turning on him. "You got a problem with that?" Reaching inside the fleece, he whipped out his letter from the Waldovian FA. Frederick took it and quickly ran his eyes over it. Luke, sitting next to him, had another look at it too. *Laog ni Tarp Taf* – it did say that on the letterhead. And the little badge in the corner *was* coloured in pink, yellow and green.

"So what d'you say now, *Cool Guy*?" Madman demanded.

Frederick calmly handed him back the letter. "I say you've been stitched up."

"What? *What?*" Madman waved the page. "It's all here in black and white!"

"And pink," gasped Half-Fat

"And yellow," wept Craig.

"And green," Chrissie giggled helplessly. *"Laog ni Tarp Taf!"*

"Are you taking my country's motto in vain?" bellowed Madman.

"No way," Cool F told him. "There's no Waldovia, man. No such place."

"No Waldovia! Naff off!" Again he brandished the letter, but already a shadow of serious doubt had crossed his features. "What about *this*?"

"Check out the date," Frederick said, with just a little smile of his own.

"April the..." Madman began, but his voice fell away to a whisper. He saw it.

"April the what?" Half-Fat managed to wheeze.

*"APRIL FOOL!"* roared everyone except Madman.

The gobsmacked goalie let the letter float to the floor. Then slowly he tore off the vile (and very expensive) green bobble-hat and hurled it at Chrissie. The YTS lad, like everyone else, was in such fits he didn't even try to defend himself – nor did he when the yellow fleece came hurtling his way. And all he kept spluttering was "*Laog ni Tarp Taf*" – and pointing at his red-faced room-mate. What did it mean?

"Try saying the whole thing back to front," Cool F suggested to everyone.

It took a while for the lower-IQ players to rearrange the letters, but finally they got there. Even Madman was smiling by now. "As it happens," he boomed over the din, "I'm well chuffed about this. It means I'm still eligible for England."

"Good thinking, son," laughed Benny, putting an arm around him. "Stranger things have happened. OK, you lot – you've had your fun! Madman's caused us all a bit of bother recently but now you've got your own back, so let that be an end to it. *This* is where it starts getting serious. We've got a team to organize here for an FA Cup semi-final on Sunday. So where do we begin?"

"With the *Laog ni Tarp Taf!*" cried every player present – including Madman.

**22**

"Aye well, this is it, lad," said Luke's grandpa. He smiled up at the magnificent red-brick Trinity Road entrance to Villa Park. "Your first Cup semi-final. Take it all in now. You never know when the next one's going to come along!"

"Oh, never mind about *semi*-finals!" said Luke's nan, proudly ruffling her grandson's hair. "He'll have the *final* to play in after this. At Wembley!"

"Nice call," grinned Terry Vaudeville, pushing through the queues to meet them. "But if you folks don't mind, I'd better get our star midfielder off to the dressing room. Cheers for delivering him. Enjoy the match."

Luke waved goodbye to his grandparents and took a last look round for Rodney and his dad, who had been planning to come together. Luke's stepdad had spun his mum a tale about an emergency client meeting in Birmingham. Luke wondered if she would notice that her pink washing-up pinny had gone too. (Rodney had worn it while watching Albion beat Villa in the Third Round – and had sworn to wear it at every tie till the Cup run was over.) But Luke saw no pink blob among the masses still outside the ground. This really was a mega-crowd.

Already Luke thought he'd seen more fans in blue and white than he'd ever seen inside Ash Acre. It was nice to have glory supporters!

Terry wouldn't let Luke stop to sign autographs or give brief interviews to all the radio and TV reporters who made a bee-line his way. "Wait till afterwards, boys!" the physio laughed. "Then he'll talk you through his winning goal!"

There seemed to be just as many people inside the great stadium as out. "This way," Terry called over his shoulder, surging through the throng with a battered old kit-bag that he'd been holding in front of him ever since meeting Luke.

"What's in that bag, Terry?" Luke asked, in the corridor leading to the dressing rooms. Twice he'd thought he had seen some sort of *movement* inside it.

Terry just cocked his head at the Aston Villa club badge on the wall. Under the crest of a lion (looking a lot more rampant than Kingsley Castle) was the single word: *Prepared.*

"Prepared," said Terry, tapping his bag and winking. "OK?"

Benny heaved his usual sigh of relief as the Boy Wonder walked in. With Luke's arrival, they were all present and correct – and looking *well* up for the big day. "Respect," Cool Frederick greeted him, tossing in a high-five. Gaffer fondly punched his arm. "We sent your mum a complimentary ticket," said Narris. "You can sit anywhere, Luke," Madman Mort told him. "Except there."

Luke turned to the corner he had nodded at in the spacious dressing room. There, hanging from one of the pegs on a length of string, was Madman's Gloster Gladiator – glued, tied, sello-taped and Elastoplasted back together! Was this a good idea? Luke shot a nervous look Benny Webb's way.

"It's OK, Luke," Mr Sheepskin assured him. "We've had a little chat. Madman really wants to have the plane there in the goal. But he's given me his word of honour that he won't hold anyone upside down if they hit it this time."

"It wouldn't be so easy with Tony Adams anyway," Dennis pointed out.

"And," Benny added, "if we let him have the plane, he's agreed not to make any engine noises before kick-off. You can't say fairer than that."

Luke smiled, hung his bag on the next peg and got into his kit as Craig gave Carl an industrial-strength leathering with the pineapple.

While Luke was doing up his trainers, there was a knock and two stars who normally played at Villa Park popped their heads round the door. The higher one belonged to ace striker Dion Dublin, the lower to club skipper and England regular Gareth Southgate.

"Just wanna wish you luck, lads," said DD. "We think you're Gunner do it!"

"Especially if it goes to pens," said Southgate, flashing his biggest grin.

"Cheers, boys," said Terry. "Oh look – there's been a mix-up." He pointed at his battered old bag, just by the door. "Someone brought that in here but it's not ours. Do us a favour and drop it into the other lot's dressing room, would you? Ask 'em to take a look inside – just in case it's theirs."

"No sweat," said Big Gareth, reaching in, picking it up and disappearing. Luke glanced at Terry, wondering what on earth he was up to. *Prepared...*

"Right then!" cried Benny. "Is everyone ready for the off? Here – if you'd like to consider them – are my personal thoughts on the ninety minutes up ahead..."

"Or a hundred and twenty," put in Chrissie. "If it goes to extra time."

"Plus however long it would take for a penalty shoot-out," added Carl.

"Yes, yes, all right," Benny nodded. "Points taken. You've all got your heads screwed on for this one, I can see. Your *Cup* heads. And you know as well as I do that no one – I mean *no one* – can touch us in the Cup. I don't care who this lot are that we're up against today. I don't care how many times they've won the Cup before. Or the League. Or the Boat Race, Grand National and London-to-Brighton Car Rally, come to that. I only know that on your day you can beat *any* bunch of overpaid Premier pillocks – even if you don't get a penny in wages for doing it. I'm pulling every string I can to get some dosh in your pockets, lads. But this, today, ain't about money. It's about glory. It's about getting to Wembley. *Now get out there and spike them Gunners!*"

They didn't need telling twice. There was no fist-shaking or silly shouting as they strode out of the dressing room and made for the tunnel. This was just eleven players, three subs, and an aeroplane that had seen a whole lot of enemy action: *all* completely focused on the job they had come here to do.

But no Arsenal team had fallen into step beside them. There at the head of the tunnel the ref was waiting to run out with his two assistants. But there was no Adams, no

Seaman, no Petit, no Overmars, no Bergkamp...

"Where are they?" Luke turned to ask an
embarrassed-looking Villa official.

"Er – it seems there was a mishap in the
dressing room. Um – there was a bag...
Apparently the whole place is infested with ...
ferrets. It's put the wind right up some of their
players. Winterburn and Dixon are still locked in
the lav."

"Well I never," said the Prepared Physio,
frowning hard to stop himself from grinning.
"But here they come now! The Arsenal, I mean
– not the ferrets." And a very white-faced Tony
Adams slowly led his men into view.

**23**

This was easily the biggest crowd Luke had ever played in front of. He hadn't even *watched* a game in a crowd this massive. Just before the ref blew his whistle to start the match, he gazed all around him at the jam-packed ground.

Oh! he thought, what it must be like to play here all time! No waterlogged pitch whenever it drizzled with rain, no floodlight failures (and look – even the lights up there were arranged in the shape of "AV"!), no tannoy breakdowns, no one taking away the tea-urn, no pay-freeze on the wages. There might, of course, be the odd ferret in the dressing room now and then, but otherwise: magnificent!

Over 40,000 people were ogling the pitch. According to Luke's grandpa, the record attendance here for a Cup match was seventy-six thousand! But that was when supporters used to stand on terraces at top grounds as well as at places like Ash Acre. Luke thought forty-odd thousand was quite enough to be going on with. And the *buzz*! It was fantastic. There couldn't possibly have been any more excitement for the World Cup games here in '66, or even for *Euro '96*.

The whole of the North Stand was awash with blue and white. And although there were masses more in red and white at the Holte End, Luke soon knew that the Albion choir, under conductor Rocky Mitford, were going to make their presence felt. As the game kicked off, the louder roars by far were rolling down from the banks of blue behind him.

The Albion team roared into action too. For the first phase of play, the wibbly-wobbly Gunners barely got a look-in. Chrissie was one hundred and fifty per cent on his game down the left flank, and Luke made sure he saw plenty of the ball. Chrissie's marker, Lee Dixon, might just as well have stayed in the loo. Big Hair turned him inside out, outside in, then twice around the houses before pinging in cross after cross that had the fabled Arsenal back four in all sorts of strife.

Once Ruel rose above Keown to bring a great fingertip save from Seaman. Then Carl did even better, beating the Jolly Mustachioed Giant only to see Adams head out from under the crossbar. And twice Cool Frederick ghosted forward, got on the end of Chrissie's crosses and laid back cushioned headers that Narris, then Half-Fat, just failed to convert.

Arsenal weren't here simply to make up the numbers, though. And Emmanuel Petit didn't get his World Cup winners' medal by sending in a stamped, addressed envelope. At last this colossal talent hit his stride and started to find Bergkamp and Anelka with a sweet stream of passes. Suddenly Albion were on the back foot and fighting to keep *their* goal intact.

But Madman – with his trusty Gloster Gladiator twirling on its string behind him – was equal to anything the men in red hurled at or across him. And after dashing out to save at the feet of Overmars, he even managed to turn the tide by feeding Luke with a throw-out from the ground. Luke found Ruel with a pinpoint fifty yard ball. Ruel back-flicked into Carl's path. And Carl's shot had goal written all over it until Seaman touched it on to his near post and away.

The crowd was still humming about that as half-time arrived. Albion too. None of them wanted to go off. Later Luke could remember nothing about the interval save the sound of Arsène Wenger shouting "Zere are *no* ferrets now!" at Nigel Winterburn who was refusing to re-enter the Arsenal dressing room.

The Division Three party-poopers picked up where they left off as the second forty-five began. The noise from the North Stand now was unbelievable. This surely was Rocky Mitford's finest hour. In between blitzes of: *"We'll Support You Evermore!" "There's Only One Lukey Green!"* and – not much got past the Supporters Club Chairman – *"Laog ni Tarp Taf!"*, Luke felt as if his hometown hordes were physically sucking the ball towards Seaman's goal.

But however often Ruel, Carl, Chrissie and Luke got into scoring positions, SuperDave and his Fab Back Four made sure the ball stayed out of the net. And then, just like in the first half, the Gunners began to fire some fearsome bullets of their own at Madman's goal. For a thrilling twenty-minute spell, the whole match seemed to turn into a one-on-one between Madman and Bergkamp. *Four* times the Dutch genius thought he'd stroked, blasted or toe-ended the ball past the Comeback Keeper. Four times Marvellous Morty somehow scrambled it away to safety. Luke had never seen the guy hit such a rich vein of form. And what a time to do it! He'd said he planned to play for England one day. On this kind of showing, who was ever going to stop him?

Then around the eighty-fourth minute mark, Luke and Frederick conjured up a fresh wave of Albion attacks. And after some desperate last-ditch Gunners defending, Ray Parlour brought down Carl Davey right on the edge of the box. Luke placed the ball for the free-kick, shaped up to aim a Beckham-esque Special high to Seaman's right – then just stood aside as Frederick powered in to drive the ball hard and low through the wall. It beat Seaman all ends up but thudded against a post. And that was that. The ref blew up for the end of ninety mins. Extra time!

Both sets of players wandered around with grim smiles for a few minutes. Arsène Wenger and Benny Webb were on the pitch, patting heads here, shaking fists there. But neither side really needed strong words or helpful hints on strategy. This was all about pride now. Pride and heart. Skill and determination. The crowd knew it. The players knew it. (The ten million TV viewers knew it too, but doubtless dear old Des and his panel were telling everyone anyway.)

So off they went again. Bergkamp v Madman. Davey v Adams. Luke v Petit. Cool F v Anelka. Individual duels all over the pitch. A titanic clash between two teams who couldn't bear the thought of coming so far but going no further.

But after fifteen minutes no one had broken the deadlock. And after changing ends yet again, and kicking off for the fourth time that afternoon, Luke saw how exhausted some of the players were looking. Not just on the Albion side either. Dixon had his socks rolled down;

Keown seemed to be struggling for breath; Anelka got such bad cramp that Wreh had to come on as sub. But Luke himself felt fresher than ever. Maybe it was because he'd played so few games recently. He still had bags of energy. And he kept getting plenty of ball.

Minute by minute – as he tore apart the tiring Arsenal defence with passes that the ailing Albion strikers were now too sluggish to reach – he began to wonder if this was meant to be *his* day. *Wait till afterwards boys*, Terry had joked with the reporters outside, *then he'll talk you through his winning goal.*..

Standing on the halfway line, Luke called for the ball from Madman. With a lightning-fast turn he left Petit for dead, nutmegged Overmars, then looked up to see Seaman five yards off his line. That was enough. On TV afterwards Mark Lawrenson couldn't get enough of the replay: "How did he chip it so far with so little backlift? It's not natural!"

But David Seaman was pretty supernatural too. Arching up high and backwards, he tipped the ball over the bar. There wasn't even time to take the corner. Three blasts from the ref's whistle brought a strange hush down on the crowd. A hundred and twenty minutes were up.

Luke shut his eyes. Fingernails all over England prepared to meet their doom. There was only one way to settle this now. It wasn't a perfect way. In many people's eyes it wasn't even fair. But by heck, as Luke's grandpa liked to say, it was the most fun any decent man could have and not get arrested.

*Penalty shoot-out!*

Benny Webb probably wasn't the best manager to have in a situation like this. The ref wanted a bit of paper from him with five names on it: the five penalty-takers – in order. But when his players dragged themselves over to the dug-out, all he had to write on was the programme. And all he had to write with was an old pencil stub from deep in a sheepskin pocket. On the glossy coloured paper, all the marks he made came out pretty well invisible.

"What are you writin' anyway, Boss?" asked Terry. "You haven't asked the lads who fancies taking one yet."

"Oh," said Benny, looking up and gaping at his eleven heroes. "Right."

"Well I'm up for one," said Gaffer Mann at once – leading by example as usual.

"Me too," said Ruel, the club's regular penalty-taker for the past two seasons.

"And me," chirped Chrissie Pick, who was sitting on the ground and massaging his sore calves. Grinning, he plucked at his shirt. "I've done a new T-shirt message under here. I wanna get a chance to show it off!"

"OK, OK, OK," said Benny to each volunteer. Nerve-wracked as he was, he knew this was all about bottle now. You couldn't *make* a player take a pen under such pressure conditions. You had to go with the guys who *wanted* it.

"Oh," said Cool F casually, after glancing first at his eager mate, "and you can put me and Luke down for a couple."

"Magic!" cried Benny, digging out a car-park ticket that he *could* write on. "I couldn't ask for a better hand than that: Mann, Bibbo, Pick, Dulac, Green. And in that order? The real heat's usually on the later takers, remember."

Luke just smiled at Frederick. "Heat's cool," they said together.

"So that's that then," Terry grinned as Benny took his ticket off to the ref. "How about you, Madman? How's it hangin'?"

Madman was calmly holding up his Gloster Gladiator by its string, inspecting it for any new signs of wear and tear. "Oh, it hangs quite nicely from the stanchions here," he replied. "Which goal are we going to be in?"

"Looks like the Holte End," Luke told him. The ref had nosed around both goalmouths and pointed to the less muddy one in front of the Arsenal fans.

"That's fine," said Madman. "Every time I save one, I'll be able to see our lot go wild in the North Stand. And I *will* save them," dreamily he patted his plane, "as long as I've got this little beauty strung up behind me."

Terry's jaw dropped. "What – for the pens as well? But you'll have to keep takin' it down when Seaman goes in, then puttin' it back up again!"

"If that's what he wants," Benny came back and cut in, "then that's what he'll do." He narrowed his eyes at Madman. "Do whatever it takes, son. *Whatever*. This is gonna be your finest hour. And when you've done the business out there I'm gonna buy you a pie so big, even Desperate Dan couldn't eat it!"

The ref blew his whistle and waved the ten pen pals and two keepers out into the centre-circle. "All the best, lads," cried Benny. "Just give it your best shot!"

Emmanuel Petit patted Luke on the back on the way out. "You played great, kid," he whispered. "*Magnifique*. Good luck now." Luke smiled and looked to see who else the Gunners were sending out. Adams, Overmars, Parlour and Bergkamp. Strong. Very strong. But they still had to beat Madman Mort.

First, though, Gaffer Mann had to beat David Seaman. The Arsenal keeper got a roof-raising cheer from the Holte End as he trotted up, waved, and turned on the line to face the Gaffer. Then the Gunners fans' noise warped into something *far* more menacing. It was like a national anthem for all the hairs on the back of Luke's neck – well, they all stood up anyway. Even before Gaffer began his run-up, their hissing, wailing, growling and spitting threatened to bring the pylons down. Gaffer just focused himself, strode in – and produced a perfect replica of David Batty's spot-kick *miss* against Argentina at *France '98*.

Seaman dived to his right. It wasn't a particularly brilliant save. It didn't have to be. But the red-and-white army behind him went bananas just the same. One kick gone and already Albion were having to play catch-up. *Not* the best start. Luke and Cool F, sitting in the centre-circle, raised an eyebrow at each other.

Ruel went to console Gaffer, who was speechless with shock. Madman meanwhile, marched into goal and, ignoring the torrent of abuse from the enemy fans, proceeded to tie his aeroplane to the stanchion. By the time he'd finished, Tony Adams was waiting, hands on hips and smiling wryly, to take his blast.

Rocky's lot in the North Stand did their best to put him off as he ran in. They needn't have bothered. Adams struck it well – full-blooded and well away from the goal's centre. But it came at a nice height and Madman, leaping right, got both gloves to it and beat it away.

"*Laog ni Tarp Taf!*" rose up from the North Stand with all the awesome turbo-power of one of Madman's best impressions. In response, he merely raised one arm, unhitched his Gloster Gladiator, then walked slowly back to high-five each of his team-mates. Concentration problems? The boy could have concentrated for England just then!

Seaman was back in position. Nil-nil after one pen each. Up stepped Ruel Bibbo: England Present v England Past. Ruel didn't take much of a run. Maybe he should have. His sidefoot shot was as perfectly-placed as ever – low, just inside the keeper's left-hand post – but not especially hard. In Div Three it would have crept in. Against a fully-extended Seaman it had no chance. *Still* nil-nil!

Madman set off on Trek Number Two. You'd have thought those Holte End throats would have given out by now. No such luck. The way they bayed as Morty did his string-and-stanchion stuff could have brought down the Great Wall of China, let alone Jericho. Yet the longish wait seemed to unnerve Emmanuel Petit, the next man up. Luke saw him frown just before he started his run. His shot went high but Madman fisted it higher – way over the bar and into the crowd. Was anyone *ever* going to trouble the keepers?

"I'd better show them how it's done, then," laughed Chrissie Pick as he stalked off to take his turn. He winked at Luke and Cool F and hoisted up his shirt just an inch. Luke wondered if he'd found a biro with Spellcheck this time.

Seaman looked a bit more nervy as the YTS lad patted his huge hair into place. Perhaps Big Dave was afraid a gob of Brylcreem might rocket off when Chrissie raced in – and slap him in the eye. Whatever the reason, the keeper flung himself right very early. It was as if he wanted to *avoid* something – like the ball, which Chrissie hit straight, hard and central. But *oh!* – lucky Arsenal!

Although Seaman knew nothing about it, the ball hit his shin and plopped down dead on the six-yard line. Chrissie screamed in, wellied it into the roof of the net, then wheeled away with his shirt already half-hoiked. But the ref was signalling no goal, and Rocky's choir's cheers died in their throats. You only get one kick in a penalty shoot-out. Five men had had theirs. Each one in vain.

Would Marc Overmars now make it a successful number six? Luke didn't think so for a minute. The sturdy little Dutchman was hopping all over the place while Madman did his bit of DIY. It was taking him longer and longer each time. Maybe, thought Luke, just possibly – *on purpose*! And The Man Who Loved Pies was thriving on all the Holte End hatred aimed his way. It seemed to be swelling him up – until he really did look as if he filled the goal.

Overmars was itching to get it over with. Madman turned and adjusted his top – making sure melancholic Marc got a flash of latex skeleton underneath. When the shot came in, high to his left, Miraculous Mr Mort plucked it from the air as coolly as if he were picking a pickled egg out of the jar on the chip-shop counter.

*"You Beauty!"* bellowed the Mitford Meistersingers. And after taking a single bow, Madman slipped the plane off its stanchion and headed back.

Luke watched Frederick rise athletically to his feet.

As little kids they'd taken loads of penalties against each other in the park. Back in those days there hadn't been any goalposts. They'd had to use two concrete pillars in the wire-mesh fence. And then they'd had to make sure they kept the ball low, or else it flew out into the road behind – and it took forever to climb over and get it.

That was then. This – Villa Park on FA Cup semi-final day – was now.

"Do it!" grinned Luke, as Cool F loped away to where David Seaman waited.

**25**

In all the discussions afterwards, Luke couldn't say he was *always* sure Cool Frederick would score.

His moment of doubt came when his mate re-settled the ball on the spot. It had rolled a fraction to the right. Just a bit of wind. But no penalty-taker on earth likes having to backtrack. And those Arsenal wall-wreckers knew it as well as anyone. *Up* went the decibel level yet again. Their deafening din was like a wall itself – a high brick wall right across Seaman's goal. Surely no one could belt a ball through that? And surely no team that was bottom of the League could *really* beat the Arsenal? Didn't that only happen in films about football? (And you didn't get much further from real life than films about football.)

Frederick straightened up and took just two steps back. From where Luke was sitting, his best friend looked dwarfed by Seaman – and a speck against the great Holte End. Cool F took one step forward. Seaman swayed just faintly to his left. Frederick noticed. As he took his next and final step, Luke could see exactly what he was going to do. He caught his breath.

Seaman's feint to the left had been a decoy. As the Cool One put boot to ball, the England man leapt right – spreading himself so wide that he seemed to cover every inch of the right-hand side of his goal. Which was all very well. But Cool F didn't hit his shot that way. Instead he gently chipped it – as smooth as a gravy sandwich – into the bottom *left*-hand corner of the net.

The wall of sound crumbled to dusty silence. Then up from the North Stand, like a massive blue-and-white hooped balloon, into the murky Midlands sky, rose the frenzied chant:

**"One-Nil To The Albion!**
**One-NIL To The Albion!"**

The chant soared on and on as Madman once again swapped places with Seaman – who was still shaking his head at the way Cool F had outsmarted him. The Arsenal faithful found their voices again when Madman took off his gloves and began to fiddle with his bit of string. Meanwhile, Dennis Bergkamp took the goalwards walk that seven men had taken, but so far only one had returned from with his mission accomplished.

The sublimely-gifted Dutch striker spun the ball in his hands, placed it, then set himself up. Luke could still hardly believe he was sharing a pitch with world-class players like this guy. Images flashed through his head of the exquisite goal he'd scored to beat Argentina – England's conquerors – at *France '98*; his unforgettable hat-trick against Leicester the season before; so *many* brilliant strikes, so many mesmerized keepers...

But Madman wasn't looking mesmerized at the moment. Busy, yes, but not mesmerized. He seemed to be having trouble with his knot. The storm of sound grew ever louder. The ref looked at his watch and yelled at Morty to get a move on. Bergkamp chewed on his lip and waited. And waited a bit more.

Then Luke noticed that Madman was fussing over his plane in a different way from usual. Instead of standing with his back to the next penalty-taker, now he was standing side-on – so that Bergkamp got a full view of his battered, beloved lucky charm. And Dazzling Dennis *was* giving it a thoroughly good eyeballing. And now, yes, he was starting to look distinctly uneasy about the thing.

Suddenly Luke realized why. Of course! Bergkamp was famously afraid of flying! So much so that he never played in Arsenal's further-flung European games because he refused to take to the air. And here was Madman making him stare at his worst nightmare: an aeroplane on the point of falling apart!

The keeper turned, but as he did so his knot slipped and the Gloster Gladiator plummeted towards the ground. With stunning reflexes Madman twisted back round and caught it – it was almost as if he'd *expected* it to fall – but not before DB had shut his eyes tight in panic. And when he opened them again, Luke could see his jaw quivering, his nostrils flaring. This was one unsettled striker.

In an instant Madman had his plane back in place. Then he took up his position on the line. Bergkamp wanted no more messing. In he strode, high and hard he hit his shot into the opposite corner from the aircraft – and openmouthed he watched as Madman launched himself into its path and turned it over the bar.

**"We're On Our Way To Wem-bley!**
**We're On Our Way To Wem-bley!"**

Rocky's raucous chorus began – even before Madman fell grinning to the ground. If there had ever been a better penalty-save, Luke hadn't seen it. He ran across with Gaffer, Ruel, Chrissie and Frederick to haul him up and hug him. (Madman was a big lad; there was enough for them all to get hold of.)

But Luke peeled away as soon as he saw Seaman return to his post. The job was not quite finished. It was indeed still one-nil to the Albion (as Rocky's lot were now informing everyone in the Greater Birmingham area). Both sides had taken four pens; both had one left. But if Luke could tuck away Albion's fifth, Arsenal needn't *bother* taking theirs. There was no way back from two-nil down.

Luke felt Gaffer pat him on the back as he headed for the spot. But in a way he *didn't* feel it. He heard the Arsenal faithful revving themselves up for one last barrage of abuse, but he didn't really hear that either. He saw David Seaman glaring straight back at him – and yet truly didn't see the brilliant keeper at all.

All he could feel was the need to hit the net. All he could hear was Terry Vaudeville telling those reporters about his winning goal. All he could see was the goal getting *bigger*, *bigger*, *BIGGER* as he swept in and struck his shot.

He had so much net to aim at. Seaman's goal was as big as the whole Nationwide League and twice as high as a Premiership striker's salary. But Luke didn't need a target that enormous. He was back in the park with Cool Frederick. He aimed to keep the ball low – so he wouldn't have to climb the wire-mesh fence and fetch it afterwards. He aimed to keep it a whisker away from the left-hand concrete pillar – where even England's Number One couldn't reach it. And he was stunningly accurate in both his aims.

He paused for a split-second to watch the ball snuggle into the net behind the utterly-beaten Seaman, then raced away into the arms first of his team-mates, then his openly weeping manager, then fifteen thousand Albion fans after a pitch invasion that all the stewards south of Sunderland couldn't have stopped.

Albion had done it! They were there! They were through to the FA Cup Final!

A great fat Ash Acre South Sider grabbed Luke from behind and plonked him on his shoulders. From up there he could see it all. Benny and Terry dancing by the dug-out like a pair of plastered puppets, then both being scooped off *their* feet as well by delirious devotees. Chrissie Pick, on Gaffer Mann's shoulders, finally showing his T-shirt to the TV cameras.

**Hair Today Wembly Tomorow!**

it proudly proclaimed. (No Spellcheck, then.)

Narris, Half-Fat, Dennis and Craig were charging around behind the North Stand goal flying a vast Union flag with *Castle Albion FC* painted in white across it. Carl and Ruel holding aloft a giant inflatable pineapple with FA Cup handles.

Then Luke felt a hand close with excruciating pain on his left ankle. "Hi, Grandpa!" he yelled down into the old boy's tear-streaked face. "What about that then?" But all Grandpa could do was shake his head in pure, proud wonder. And all Luke's nan could do was kiss Luke's *right* ankle – again and again and again and again.

"Far out, man! Far *out*!" came a cry behind him. Luke twisted round to see his dad locked in a clinch with Rodney – all pink pinny, with his glasses askew.

"*We 'ad 'em!*" screamed the mild-mannered bird-fancier, gripping Luke's dad tighter and bouncing up and down with him. "*We done the flippin' Gunners!*"

Then Luke's trusty steed headed over towards the tunnel. Madman Mort, cradling his plane, was also heading that way – held up by a score of fans who, even so, looked as if they were beginning to feel the weight. Luke reached across and high-fived the hero. Then he felt a tap on his back, turned, and found himself high-fiving the only man in Villa Park wearing Raybans. (Presumably he had paid the two fans underneath to hold *him* shoulder-high too.)

"Super stuff, Luke," shouted Agent Veal. "And you, Madman. This will send your market value through the roof. Let's do post-match champagne-supper!"

"Hey!" roared Benny Webb, riding up on his own sea of shoulders, pushing Veal only lightly but sending him crashing to the turf. "You can forget about champagne suppers. I'm buying him the biggest cow pie he's ever seen!"

Madman frowned. "Cow pie?" he yelled back thoughtfully. "Hmmm. What I *really* fancy is a KFC Party Bucket with a job-lot of Pot Noodles on the side."

"KFC! Pot Noodles! After winning an FA Cup semi-final!" cried the ref as *he* was carried past by some obviously-confused fans. "Are you completely *mad*?"

"*YEAH!*" replied what sounded like every single voice in the stadium, "*HE IS!*"

**Paul Stewart**

### Football Mad

2-1 up in the inter-school cup final, captain Gary Connell finds the net ... at the wrong end! Now cup glory rests on a tricky replay...

### Football Mad 2

*Offside!*

The inter-school cup is up for grabs again. But Craig won't be playing. He's been dropped – and he's not happy...

### Football Mad 3

*Hat-trick!*

Could it be cup-final number three? Goalkeeper Danny is in trouble. New team coach Mr Carlton has really got it in for him...

# Creatures

## The Series With Bite!

Everyone loves animals. The birds in the trees. The dogs running in the park. That cute little kitten.

But don't get too close. Not until you're sure. Are they ordinary animals – or are they creatures?

### 1. Once I Caught a Fish Alive
Paul's special new fish is causing problems. He wants to get rid of it, but the fish has other ideas...

### 2. If You Go Down to the Woods
Alex is having serious problems with the school play costumes. Did that fur coat just move?

### 3. See How They Run
Jon's next-door neighbour is very weird. In fact, Jon isn't sure that Frankie is completely human...

### 4. Who's Been Sitting in My Chair?
Rhoda's cat Opal seems to be terrified ... of a chair! But then this chair belongs to a very strange cat...

*Look out for these new creatures...*

### 5. Atishoo! Atishoo! All Fall Down!
Chocky the mynah bird is a great school pet. But now he's turning nasty. And you'd better do what he says...

### 6. Give a Dog a Bone
A statue of a faithful dog sounds really cute. But this dog is faithful unto death. And beyond...

# Creatures – you have been warned!

# HURRICANE HAMISH
## Mark Jefferson

### HURRICANE HAMISH
#### THE CALYPSO CRICKETER

Hurricane Hamish has always been a bit special – ever since he was found washed up on a Caribbean beach wrapped in an MCC towel. He's only twelve, but he can bowl fast. Really fast. So fast he might be about to play for the West Indies...

### HURRICANE HAMISH
#### THE CRICKET WORLD CUP

Hurricane Hamish is back – and now he's in England, determined to help the West Indies win the Cricket World Cup. But England is so cold! The grounds are so wet and slippery that Hurricane can't even stay standing, let alone bowl fast...

*"The ideal literary companion for this summer's Carnival of Cricket – the World Cup."*
Lord MacLaurin, Chairman of the England and Wales Cricket Board

*"Mark Jefferson has scored a real winner with Hurricane Hamish ... this pacey romp of a book."*
Christina Hardyment, The Independent

*"A novel which, like its hero, has pace and heart."*
Nicolette Jones, The Sunday Times